In the SHADOWS of ROME

The
MYSTERIOUS
GOBLET

Cover illustration: William Bonhotal

Under the direction of Romain Lizé, CEO, MAGNIFICAT
Editor, MAGNIFICAT: Isabelle Galmiche
Editor, Ignatius: Vivian Dudro
Proofreaders: Kathleen Hollenbeck, Samuel Wigutow
Layout Designers: Élisabeth Hebert, Magali Meunier
Layout: Text'Oh (Dole)
Production: Thierry Dubus, Sabine Marioni

In the SHADOWS of ROME

The MYSTERIOUS GOBLET

Sophie de Mullenheim

Translated by
Janet Chevrier

MAGNIFICAT · Ignatius

CONTENTS

Do you think that I have come
to establish peace on the earth?
No, I tell you, but rather division.
From now on a household of five
will be divided, three against two
and two against three.
Luke 12:51-52

PROLOGUE

Roman Hispania, A.D. 303

Lurking in the woods, hidden behind a tree, he kept his eyes fastened on the door of the little house. This was it. He had been searching for three days, but now he was sure the goal of his mission was there within those four walls. All that remained was to be patient and wait until the time was right.

Suddenly, he stiffened; someone had just moved inside the house. His face lit up. A steely glint flashed in his beady eyes. His thin lips pinched into a cold, sneering smile.

People called him Delitilis, "the cleaner," the man who tidies up awkward evidence, who gets rid of an embarrassing witness, who removes a troublesome enemy, or... people pay him to make things go away. Cleanly. Coolly. Some people produce, make things, create. Delitilis wipes out, obliterates, eliminates. He's never been known to fail, to show any weakness. No one really knows who he is or where he comes from. He travels all over Hispania, in Gaul too, and sometimes all the way to Rome. When someone needs him, he turns up as if by magic. Some people think he's a bit of a sorcerer. He inspires respect, but above all terror. Even those who call on his services fear him.

A silhouette appeared in the doorway of the little house. Then a second, smaller figure joined him. Delitilis squinted. Yes, that was his man. And by his side, that must be his little girl. Delitilis had been informed that, since the death of the man's wife, he had been bringing her up on his own. The man stopped a moment on the doorstep, straightened his little girl's clothes, and then took her by the hand and came out. Delitilis followed his every movement. He watched him close the door behind him, look up at the sky, and slowly walk away from the house. It was time. Delitilis had to act fast.

As soon as the man was out of sight, Delitilis sprang forward. He crossed the little courtyard with such a rapid, light step, his feet hardly touched the ground. He plastered himself against the wall of the house and waited a few moments, on the lookout. He slipped around to the window at the back of the house and waited. There wasn't a sound. The coast was clear. Delitilis gripped the club in his hand a little more tightly. His look hardened. He repeated to himself what he had to do: slip through the window, get the casket, make his getaway, and destroy it. If everything went according to plan, it shouldn't take more than a few minutes. A purse full of money for such a simple job! No one had ever paid him that well.

"The family of a certain Lorenzo, who died in Rome in A.D. 258, the son of Orencio y Paciencia, lives near Huesca. They have a wooden casket. Destroy it!"

That's all his clients had told him. But that was enough for Delitilis to step in. And that was how he liked to work: the less he knew the better. No need to get bogged down in details and emotions.

Delitilis hoisted himself up in one quick movement. Once inside the only room in the house, his attention was immediately caught by a large trunk placed against the wall on the right. It was the only piece of furniture in the room, except for a mattress lying on the floor and a few cushions and pieces of pottery. Delitilis went up to it, laid his club on the floor, and opened the trunk. If the casket really was in this house, as he suspected, this is where it must be hidden. He felt through the linens a few pieces of tableware.

Very quickly, his fingers came in contact with a rough edge sticking out. A little casket in dark wood, polished with the years, was hidden right at the bottom. Delitilis slipped it into the canvas bag slung around his shoulder, put everything carefully back in place so no one would suspect he had been there, picked up his club, and slipped out the window as nimbly as he had entered. Once back in the safety of the shady wood where he had earlier kept a lookout, he breathed a sigh of relief and satisfaction. All he had to do now was destroy the casket and it would be mission accomplished.

Delitilis sat the small wooden box on a flat rock and raised his heavy club. He was about to smash it to smithereens when he recalled the words his clients had whispered to one another as they were taking leave of him: "Have you ever seen what's inside the box?"

Almost despite himself, Delitilis stopped, club in mid-air. It lasted only a few seconds but, for the first time in his life, he felt a whole new sensation: curiosity. He who was usually so cool and methodical longed to see what was inside the box. It wasn't just the words of his client that were bothering him. Why had he been paid so much for such an apparently simple job? Delitilis lowered his arm and laid his club on the ground. He picked the lock and slowly opened the lid.

What a disappointment!

There was no treasure in the box.

Nothing but a simple goblet made of brown stone.

I

THE GOSSIP

At first, some thought it was a joke. It was so improbable. Others feared it was malicious gossip spread to trap the interested parties. After all, the story had all the features that arouse idle curiosity.

Then, slowly but surely, the rumor was confirmed. Nothing official, but it was an open secret. From the dark side streets to the crypts, from the crypts to the backrooms of shops, from the backrooms to the catacombs, from the catacombs to little alleyways, people cautiously whispered. They whispered, looking over their shoulders for fear of being overheard.

"It's in Rome!"

Other, braver souls dared to say they had seen it. Most of the time, they were lying, but how could you blame them? The news was so amazing, so unhoped-for. And a little terrifying too.

II

STALKED!

Delitilis slightly quickened his pace. He had already spotted the man following him a moment ago—a tall man with an athletic build, square-shouldered and square-jawed. And a very dark complexion. One of his eyelids drooped, almost as though one eye were closed. The streets of Rome were packed, and anyone else but Delitilis wouldn't have noticed a thing. But you don't spend a lifetime in crime without developing a kind of sixth sense about danger. Delitilis had already come across that man the day before. He was sure of it. And perhaps even one time before that.

Hidden under his tunic, Delitilis clasped the goblet to his chest. He had to get it to his client. If it weren't for this man on his tail, he would have already handed it over—and would now be rich. Enormously rich. His client had offered him a fortune for the goblet he brought back from Hispania. But he had promised to be discreet. No one must know who they were. No one must suspect them of possessing the goblet. Delitilis couldn't go to them with this villain on his heels.

Delitilis scanned the crowd. He needed to find a safe place to hide the unwieldy object until he could throw his pursuer off his tail. He couldn't risk losing the goblet, breaking it, or, even worse, having it stolen—not after all these months of searching for it.

Suddenly, Delitilis spotted three boys just about to enter one of the posh houses on the street. They clearly lived there, so he could easily find them again. Without hesitation, he walked up to them, noting every detail of their appearance.

The tallest one was massive, a black-skinned giant with frizzy hair. "Surely a slave," thought Delitilis, making a mental note. The one next to him couldn't be more different. Small, thin, and very pale, with blond, almost white, hair. In spite of his puniness, he had extraordinary energy, judging by his lively movements and confident gestures. But it was hard to say how old he might be—eleven? fifteen? His body was that of a child, but his face looked like that of a young adult. Finally, the third boy must be about fourteen. He had curly chestnut hair, a smiling face, and a monkey perched on his shoulder. Delitilis smiled on seeing the little animal. That was an easy mark of identification: it wasn't every day in Rome, or anywhere else for that matter, that you saw a kid with a monkey.

"Excuse me," Delitilis said to the boys in a polite voice. "I see you live around here... Could you help me?"

The boy with the monkey turned to him with a friendly smile and asked, "How can we help you?"

"I'm not from Rome," Delitilis explained, drawing nearer to the boys, "and this city is so big. Can you tell me the way to the Forum?"

"The Forum! Nothing simpler..." The boy then rattled off a long, involved set of directions, which were anything but simple.

Delitilis moved closer to him and bent forward to follow his every gesture. He feigned concentration, but his attention was elsewhere. He was looking for a way to stash the goblet safely in the boy's clothing. At one point, he leaned so close to the boy, he almost lost his balance and caught hold of the boy's cloak to steady himself.

"Oh, excuse me," Delitilis apologized. "I'm very tired from my travels."

The little monkey fidgeted nervously on the boy's shoulder. Delitilis took a step back and repeated the directions as he looked around him. His pursuer had also stopped, pretending to be interested in a market stall across the street. Delitilis suddenly stood up straight. The stall keeper began a sales pitch to his pursuer. It was the moment for Delitilis to disappear.

"Thank you, thanks so much," he said to the boy. "I'm sure I can find it now."

And without another word, he suddenly moved off at a fast clip.

"Hey, wait a minute!" the boy called after him. "It's not that way..."

That made no difference to Delitilis, who kept going in the wrong direction. And the further away he got, the faster he went.

"Unbelievable!" exclaimed Titus, turning to his two friends. "My directions were perfectly clear."

Maximus, the smallest of the three, smiled. "Couldn't have been any clearer," he said with amusement. "Isn't that right, Aghiles?"

The huge slave nodded his head but said nothing. Of the three of them, he was the only one who had noticed that someone immediately followed the man who had asked for directions.

III

A MISTAKE?

"How about a little something to eat?" Titus suggested as he closed the door behind him. "I'm starving."

Dux danced on his shoulder, smacking his lips with delight.

"Oh, stop it, Dux; I wasn't talking to you. All this monkey thinks about is food!"

Maximus and Aghiles stepped into the house before him and entered the open-air atrium with its central fountain. A nice little meal would be just the thing. They had spent the morning tending to the animals of Titus' father—cleaning out the dirty litter, carrying in clean straw, and lugging in sides of beef for the tigers, seeds for the birds, and bundles of leaves for the elephants. Their hands were covered in blisters, and their muscles ached. Even Aghiles was blistered and sore, and he was used to manual labor.

Ever since Titus' father, Flavius Octavius, had brought back a lion for the emperor,[1] his reputation as a wild animal trader grew greater than ever, and his business expanded too. People flocked from all over asking him for animals—giraffes, crocodiles, hippos, ostriches... Rich Romans vied for originality in their orders in an attempt to wow the guests at their dinner parties. For in Rome, the members of the upper class liked to

---

1. See volume 2, *A Lion for the Emperor.*

entertain extravagantly, to show off their wealth. No expense was spared on their silverware, furniture, fine wines, abundant food, and now, exotic animals. They displayed their possessions unreservedly, with pride, but above all as a courtesy. It was unthinkable to receive a guest without doing him the honor of offering the best.

This new flood of orders meant a boom in trade for Titus' father, who was already very busy. Business was thriving. He had lots of people to help him: several hired hands and slaves busied themselves tending to the animals. But he could still never afford to turn down an offer of help from his son and his friends, especially when he was away for a few days on business trips, as was the case now. Flavius Octavius secretly hoped that by becoming involved in the business, Titus would want to take over the family enterprise one day. After all, in three years, his son would come of age. What father wouldn't feel the same? If only Titus weren't so timid...

Titus unbuckled his leather belt with its large pouch attached. When he laid it on a stool in the atrium, it gave a thud.

"What...?" said Titus with surprise. "What did I put in there?"

He picked up his belt and opened the pouch.

"What in the world...?"

In his pouch was a brown goblet he had never seen before.

"Maximus, is this yours?"

"No."

"Aghilès?"

The slave shook his head.

The three boys examined the goblet. It looked like agate, a very hard stone, streaked with orange. Agate was a rare stone, little used in Rome, and even less so for tableware, which was most often made of pottery or, for the wealthiest people, of silver or another metal.

"Maybe someone gave it to you at your father's office?" Maximus suggested.

"But I would remember that. Unless..." Titus had an idea. "That man just now," he began.

"What man?"

"The one who asked for directions."

"He gave you this goblet?"

"No, that's not what I mean, but..." Titus shook his head.

"But what? Go on," Maximus urged him.

"Don't you think he was a little odd?" Titus asked.

Maximus shrugged his shoulders, "What was so odd about him?"

"He grabbed hold of me, as though he were about to fall over. Even Dux didn't like it."

As Maximus and Aghiles remained silent, Titus went on. "And then, he left in exactly the opposite direction I told him to go."

"Well, for a stranger to Rome, your directions were far from clear."

"But he gave the impression he understood them very well."

"He was just being polite."

Aghiles asked, "And you think he might have taken advantage of the moment to slip this into your pouch?"

"Why not?" Titus said, nodding, relieved that his friend had come to the same conclusion he had.

"But why would he do that?" Maximus doubtfully asked. He was convinced Titus had simply forgotten where he had picked up the goblet.

"Because he was being followed!" said Aghiles.

IV

THE CHASE

Delitilis continued at a quick pace. He didn't need to look behind him to see that his pursuer was still on his tail. He simply knew it. Above all, he mustn't run. Not now. He had to keep a cool head. As he hurried on, Delitilis tried to work out where he had made a mistake. Because if a man was tailing him, it must be because he had slipped up somewhere.

To be honest, Delitilis knew very well when things had started to go wrong. It was so obvious, he wondered how he hadn't realized it from the start. He had never, not once, failed to complete a mission. He had never weakened when the time came to strike, never hesitated to set fire to a house, never shrunk from stealing, murdering, lying, attacking. So why this time, for the first time in his life, had he given in to the temptation of curiosity? And why, once his curiosity was satisfied, hadn't he simply destroyed the goblet as he had been asked to do? If only his greed hadn't got the better of him.

Once over his disappointment at the sight of this goblet, Delitilis wondered why his clients were in such a rush to destroy it, why they had offered him such a big payoff. Doubts started creeping into his mind. There must be something else behind this goblet; it must be a treasure or the key to some secret. He could surely make money out of it, much, much more money than he ever had. The prospect of it made him rejoice. Rich at last!

His intuition had been right after all. The man following him seemed to prove that the goblet was indeed precious. Delitilis would milk the competing passions it unleashed for all they were worth. He could increase the price by playing one bidder off another. This job now become a game for him. At last, he was on the point of handing over the object for an astronomically indecent amount. But he hadn't anticipated the endgame would be so difficult. And now that he felt things starting to turn against him, he was in a hurry to get it all over with.

Delitilis looked for the best place to slip out of sight of his pursuer. He considered going to the Forum to melt into the huge crowd. But, in the end, he thought that was too risky. It would be too difficult to circulate among all the passersby and the merchants. He didn't like the idea, either, of turning back and running the risk of encountering his pursuer again. Better to stay on a main road with lots of little side streets to the right and left.

At a run, he would have no trouble shaking off the man on his heels. He was small, wiry, and extremely muscular while his pursuer was tall and thickly built. At least Delitilis had managed to put the goblet in a safe place. That boy hadn't suspected a thing, and even when he did find the object in his sack, he wouldn't know what it was. Delitilis had noted a few of the details of the house. He was sure he would have no trouble finding it again.

Several yards behind Delitilis, Tiburtius concentrated harder than ever. "I've almost got him," he thought, clenching his huge fists.

This long manhunt was starting to wear him out, and if the stakes weren't so high, he would have given up long ago. But he had to be absolutely sure of getting that goblet before it once again disappeared or fell into the wrong hands.

Suddenly, Tiburtius strained forward. Delitilis had just turned down a side street. He was about to escape! Tiburtius redoubled his pace. There was no question of letting the man get away now. Tiburtius rushed into the side street and spotted Delitilis as he disappeared into another street a little farther away. Tiburtius ran as fast as he could, but he was gasping for air. His heart was pounding. His legs were giving out.

When Tiburtius turned onto the street where Delitilis had disappeared, he stopped in dismay. The road was wide and crowded with stalls and shoppers—the perfect place to disappear from view. It was no use looking over the heads of the crowd; Tiburtius could see no one walking a little too fast, no one who looked like the man who had just slipped through his fingers.

"Ha, child's play!" Delitilis smugly thought to himself as he secretly watched his pursuer. He had slipped into a draper's shop from where he could keep an eye on the street through the fabric hanging on display in the window. The man following him desperately cast his eye up and down the street. Delitilis could tell he had lost his trail.

Getting rid of this man hadn't been difficult, but Delitilis' satisfaction was short-lived. He wasn't yet in control of the situation. Despite all his precautions, he had been spotted. He realized that he must retrieve the goblet and get paid for it as soon as possible—no fishing around for better offers.

This evening, he decided, he would go back to the house of that boy who had given him directions. He would get that goblet back, even if he had to use force. Then he would take it right to his client's home. Once the money was in his pocket, he would disappear for a while. This chase through the streets of Rome made it clear to him that he wasn't the same careful, efficient man he used to be.

V

BE BRAVE!

It has to be said, Titus wasn't brave. Or, rather, he *was* brave as long as he wasn't in any danger. To hear him talk, he was afraid of nothing and no one. But as soon as it was a matter of putting his words into action, he either hid or took to his heels.

The goblet hidden in his bag by that man on the run frightened him. Surely the man would return for it. And what would he do to Titus? Kill him? What about his pursuers? Might they also want to kill Titus if they find out he has the goblet? Might they also be capable of torture? What if they asked him questions he couldn't answer? They probably wouldn't believe that he didn't know anything and then torture him for information. Just the thought of what could happen to him made Titus tremble.

"Take the goblet home with you," he suggested to Maximus.

"But what if that man comes back here to get it?"

"I'll tell him that you've got it."

Maximus gave him a wry smile. "And you'll give him my address, will you?"

"Of course," Titus exclaimed.

"Charming. If I understand correctly, you'll let me take all the risk."

Titus shook his head. "It's not that… I mean, it's just that you, you have Aghiles."

"And...?"

"He's big and strong. He'll protect you."

"That's just what I'm saying, Titus. You're happy to let me take all the risk."

Titus gave a nervous little laugh. "What risk?" he said. "We have no proof that what Aghiles says is true."

"In that case, you keep the goblet."

Titus gave a broad smile. "I know! You just need to stay here tonight. Since my parents are away for several days, you can keep me company."

Maximus and Aghiles shot each other an amused glance. That Titus always had an answer for everything.

"Okay," Maximus nodded.

"Okay? You agree?!" Titus repeated, unable to hide his surprise that his friend gave in so easily.

"I'd never forgive myself if anything happened to you," replied Maximus with gravity. "Or if you were to solve this mystery on your own," he thought to himself, for his curiosity was indeed piqued. If what Aghiles said was true, the man was very likely to return for his goblet in the coming hours. And Maximus wanted to be there when he did.

VI

A BIT OF A SETBACK

"What an idiot!" Delitilis cursed himself as he walked up and down the street. At this time of day, now that it was dark, he couldn't get his bearings. The street was almost deserted. The shops were closed, and the crowd had left the thoroughfare. The light was different; nothing looked the same as it had a few hours ago. What's worse, all the housefronts looked identical. Delitilis thought he had noted a few distinct details, but now he noticed the same things on several other houses. For example, he remembered a mosaic above the entrance. But nearly all the houses in the street had one. And Delitilis couldn't remember what it depicted. A scene of daily life? The gods? An illustration of a trade?

Delitilis advanced slowly, examining every portico, trying to find a detail that would give him a lead, something that looked familiar, the slightest thing. He didn't care how long it took him—he had to get that goblet back. He hadn't gone through all this only to fall at the last hurdle.

From within the walls of the villas, he could sometimes hear voices and loud laughter. He tried to make out a particular voice, but that was hopeless. He had only talked to that boy for a few moments. And only one of the boys had spoken.

Delitilis was even more tenacious in his search than usual. All his senses were on the alert. He looked for anything that might put him on the scent of those three boys. Suddenly, he stopped. As he approached the entrance to one house, he felt a familiar feeling, the same sort of jumpiness that had gripped him when he had realized he was being followed. Delitilis trusted his instincts. If he felt like this, perhaps it was because he had returned to the place he had been earlier that day.

He turned around. The street was empty. There was another street in front of him—perhaps the one he had turned down before. The market stalls were closed. How to recognize the one where his pursuer had been earlier?

"It must be here," he thought.

But when he looked at the wall above the front door, there was no mosaic.

Delitilis shook his head and ground his teeth. He had to hold back a scream of rage. Idiot! Fool! He had no words to describe how stupid he had been. He didn't recognize himself anymore, couldn't understand how this could have happened. It really was time to put an end to all this. Otherwise, it would be the end of him. He set off again, more determined than ever. He had to find that house!

At last he stopped in front of a house that looked familiar to him. It had a mosaic above the doorway, but this one was different from the others. There were wild animals—lions, elephants, buffalos, and... a monkey! Delitilis smiled. That monkey was the clue he had been searching for. It reminded him of the animal perched on the shoulder of that boy. When Delitilis turned to look around, he noticed a market stall across the street. It all added up.

He stepped back from the house to consider how he could break in. He noted the size of the windows and the height to the rooftop terrace. He identified all the footholds for climbing the walls, and the doorways. He quickly forgot his earlier setbacks as the adrenaline pumping through his veins made him quiver. He almost felt like his old self again. After all, he was Delitilis, the cleaner.

He was almost his old self, but not completely, because the old Delitilis would already have spotted and put out of commission the massive shadow approaching him.

VII

A SINISTER DISCOVERY

The first glimmers of dawn filtered through the shutters. Maximus blinked several times as if to chase away the frail rays of morning light. He turned gently on his side and looked at Titus, who was sleeping soundly. Maximus smiled with amusement. Titus, who had been so worried just a few hours before, was now dead to the world.

Aghiles was lying on his back with his eyes wide open. Maximus knew his slave and friend, like him, hadn't slept a wink. Without a word to each other, they had both fought off sleep to stay on the lookout and take the man by surprise whenever he might appear. If he did appear.

But he hadn't come. Maximus was almost disappointed.

Maximus watched the motes of dust dancing in the sunlight just above Titus' nose. In a few moments, the sun would knock at the door of his friend's eyelids and wake him up. In the meantime, the little particles were transformed into sequins sparkling in the sun. A light breeze sent them pirouetting here and there. A few flecks of dust settled on the tip of Titus' nose. His nostrils twitched a bit. Then his nose wrinkled, and all of a sudden: "Atchoo!"

The sneeze woke Titus, who sat up in his bed. It took him a few seconds to gather his wits and recognize Maximus and Aghiles, who had stayed overnight.

"Did I just sneeze?" he asked.

Maximus nodded and said, "Indeed you did."

Titus went pale. "That's a bad omen," he whispered.

Maximus winced. Without a doubt, Titus was one of the most superstitious people he knew. He interpreted everything as a sign, good or bad, organized his day according to the omens, and worriedly looked out for messages from the gods. According to him, waking up with a sneeze was the promise of a bad day. It was sure to be a bad day for Maximus and Aghiles because whenever Titus believed that the gods were against him, it was almost impossible to make him see sense. He would grumble, make dire predictions, and refuse to take even the slightest risk.

As Titus was shaking his head over the evil fate that had awakened him with a sneeze, a woman's cry broke the silence of the house. It was a bloodcurdling scream of terror. Maximus and Aghiles jumped from their beds. Careful to get out of bed on his right foot—so he wouldn't further jinx his day—Titus rose quickly too. The three friends ran to the atrium around which all the different rooms of the house were arrayed. In the *vestibulum*,[1] a woman seized with nervous trembling was staring at the open front door. Two slaves came rushing in, muffling curses.

"What's going on?" demanded an old man, who came limping behind them with a worried look.

With Flavius Octavius and his wife away on a business trip, old Faustus had been placed in charge of the household. It was hard to say how old he was; he had been in the service of Flavius Octavius for years.

Faustus held a special status in the household of Flavius Octavius. He entered his master's service as a slave, but some years ago Flavius Octavius rewarded his diligence and loyalty

---

1. The main entrance hall of a Roman house.

by giving him his freedom. Free to leave the household, Faustus could have left to start a new life. But he didn't. With no ties outside the family of his master, he remained with Flavius Octavius, who entrusted him with more and more responsibilities. The trust between the two men was total, and it wasn't unusual for Titus' father to ask his old friend's advice before making a decision.

As Faustus was highly esteemed by Flavius Octavius and his family, he in turn treated all the slaves of the household with respect. And they looked up to him as a role model, a sort of patriarch who treated them firmly but fairly.

"What's going on?!" Faustus repeated as he approached the *vestibulum*. When he got to the door, he froze. "By Jupiter!" he said.

"What is it?" Titus asked, rushing forward with Maximus and Aghiles on his heels.

Faustus turned around and stopped him with an abrupt gesture. "Come no further!" he ordered him. "There's no need for you to see this."

But it was too late. Titus gave a start as, through the open door, he saw a body lying on the front step. He went pale and took a step back. Then Maximus and Aghiles saw the body too.

A slave knelt down beside the man and placed his fingers on his neck. After a few seconds, he raised his head and somberly pronounced, "He's dead."

Behind Faustus, the woman who first saw the dead man stifled another cry.

"Bring her a glass of wine to calm her," Faustus ordered. Then he went out the door and leaned over the body himself. "Poor man," he said.

The body was stretched out, face down, with a thin cord around his neck that had left a deep red gash.

"He's been strangled," Faustus said. "Turn him over."

The two slaves bent down, one at his head, the other at his feet. They grasped the body firmly and turned it over in one movement. They couldn't help a violent step backward on seeing the purplish face, the bloodshot eyes still wide open in surprise, the twisted mouth, and the blue lips.

Faustus, too, averted his eyes. Then, slowly, he again looked at the victim to study his features. He pursed his lips. He didn't recognize this face at all. And yet he knew better than anyone those who had business with the household, had dealings with Flavius Octavius, or lived in the neighborhood. The old man never forgot a face.

"Do any of you know who he is?" he asked.

The men around him shook their heads.

"So it's not some message or a threat," Faustus replied, not without some relief. Faustus knew Flavius Octavius had many enemies who resented his success and would be only too happy for an occasion to get rid of him or cause his downfall. There had been much fierce business rivalry lately.

Faustus had almost forgotten about Titus, Maximus, and Aghiles, who out of morbid curiosity craned their necks to see the man's face. Titus went white. His legs gave way. He collapsed to the floor with a dull thud. He looked as though he couldn't breathe. Next to him, Maximus and Aghiles froze.

"I thought I told you to keep back!" thundered Faustus.

"That... that man," Titus stammered. "That man... he's..." He couldn't get another word out.

His father's old servant looked at him suspiciously. "Do you know him?" he asked.

Titus was unable to speak. It was all he could do to give a little nod of the head.

"Yes, we've seen him before," Maximus intervened. "We came across him here, at your door, yesterday afternoon."

VIII

THE RUMOR MILL

All this hubbub at the door of Flavius Octavius' house quickly drew the attention of the early morning passersby. At that hour, there wasn't usually much going on, so people were naturally attracted to the commotion. They jostled one another trying to get a better view.

"Move those people away," Faustus ordered the slaves. "Don't let them come any closer."

But the household staff struggled to contain the crowd. The more they pushed them back, the more they attracted other curious onlookers.

"Call the *urbaniciani*!"[1] Faustus shouted.

The first arrivals with the best view were spreading the news to those behind them. Word rapidly spread that a man had been murdered in front of the house of the famous wild-animal trader.

"Who is it?"

"Can you see anything?"

"Do you know who it is?"

A murder? What luck! What better for making conversation at the barber shop later? But tongues were already wagging.

---

1. A kind of municipal police force.

People were already embellishing on what they had seen and heard.

"He was stabbed to death! Five stab wounds!"

"No, three!"

"He was mutilated!"

"Someone said he was strangled!"

"Oooh... ahhh!"

The identity of the victim remained a mystery, but it would take more than that to stop the wild speculation of the public.

"Someone said the man came from the Forum."

"He's an escaped prisoner."

"No, it's surely one of Flavius Octavius' customers."

"Did he have debts?"

"Who knows."

Rumors were flying. People gave each other knowing looks. Faustus could do without this unfortunate publicity for his master, but he could do nothing to stop the gossip. He had no idea who the victim was or what he was doing on the doorstep of the house. And he couldn't hold back the advancing crowd.

If he tried to defend himself, he too would become a suspect. But if he said nothing, they would think he had something to hide. It was a no-win situation. His only chance was to get to the bottom of the matter with the help of the Roman police, who would be there any minute. He just hoped they would know the identity of this man with the bad manners to get himself killed right on his doorstep. He counted on them to sort out the affair quickly so that, by the time his master returned, it would all be only a bad memory.

In the meanwhile, the neighbors spun tales of their own.

"Did you see the look on the face of Flavius Octavius' son?"

"Titus?"

"Yes, Titus. He's Flavius Octavius' only son."

"So?"

"He almost fainted when he saw the body."

"Well, that's normal. He's young. And it isn't a pretty sight."

"I think they must have known each other."

"Who?"

"Titus and the victim."

"No... It's not possible..."

"Someone saw them together."

"Where?"

"I don't know."

"When?"

"Yesterday... or maybe a little earlier this week."

"They must have been friends."

Not far from the house, a tall, strongly built man was mingling with the crowd. But unlike the others, he wasn't straining to see—just trying to listen, to hear what people were saying and gather information. The evening before, when he had searched Delitilis' body, he had found nothing on him.

"They must have been friends," he repeated to himself. "Now that's interesting..."

IX

A MYSTERIOUS GOBLET

"The key to it all lies here," said Maximus, as he examined the goblet Titus had found in his bag the day before.

The noise at the street door was slowly simmering down. The gossip continued but had moved away from the windows of the villa. Now it was spreading through the city, embroidered with new more or less outlandish details at every street corner. Four men, sent by the Roman guard, had arrived a little while ago. They managed to push back the curiosity-seekers and keep them at a distance from the house of Flavius Octavius. They had been ordered to remove the body and establish a cordoned-off zone that no one could cross.

"Are you telling me I don't have the right to leave the house?" Faustus exclaimed to the captain of the guard.

"Not until further orders."

"But I didn't kill that man!"

"Until we have an idea of who did, no one goes in or out of the villa."

"You surely don't suspect me!" shouted the old man with indignation.

"No more than I suspect any of the other inhabitants of this house or the Roman citizens in the street."

Maximus, Titus, and Aghiles took refuge in Titus' bedroom as they awaited questioning. Titus was quivering in a corner, terrified. He hadn't spoken a word since the discovery of the body. His eyes were wide open, staring straight in front of him, because as soon as he closed them, all he could see was the face of the dead man, his twisted mouth, his blank eyes. Then, slowly, the image would shift, and it was his face instead of that of the corpse. If that man had been killed trying to retrieve the goblet, that meant Titus himself was now in mortal danger!

Maximus turned the goblet back and forth in his hands. But however hard he looked, he could find nothing special about it. Yes, the stone was pretty and beautifully honed, but there was nothing to make it particularly valuable—no gold or silver or jewels. It wasn't very big, only a few inches deep, carved in agate with a lip around the edge. It was tan but took on a brownish-orangey tinge in the light. No doubt it was a piece of everyday tableware belonging to some dignitary or another.

"Who would kill for a goblet like this?" he asked.

Titus shivered at the question. He moaned.

Maximus looked at his speechless friend and asked, "Titus, are you all right?"

No response.

"Pull yourself together! They're about to question us."

Still no answer. Titus just kept staring straight before him, as though he had lost his reason.

"Come on, Titus! Snap out of it!"

Maximus went to Titus and passed his hand in front of his face. Nothing. Titus didn't blink an eye.

Disturbed by this lack of reaction, Maximus warned him, "Come on, don't make me use force..."

When Titus still remained vacant, Maximus slapped him. Titus swayed a bit, sat up again, and went on staring straight in front of him as his cheek turned scarlet.

"This isn't funny anymore, Titus," Maximus said with a sigh.

Still nothing. Titus didn't even respond when Dux jumped on his head and pulled his hair. The little monkey instinctively knew something was wrong with his master. In his own way, he was trying to get a reaction.

There was knock at the door—one sharp, loud rap. This time, Titus gave a start, but then he huddled up even more into a ball. Maximus quickly slipped the goblet under his tunic.

A man entered the room, followed by Faustus. The man was tall, muscular, with curly blond hair, a round nose, small bright eyes, and thick lips—an almost cherubic face on the body of an athlete.

"Titus, Maximus, Aghiles," Faustus said to the boys, "this is Septimus Demetrius, chief of the *urbaniciani* in charge of the investigation. He is going to question you. I told him that you know the victim. He wants you to tell him everything you know about him. I would be grateful for your full cooperation. He needs your help in his inquiries."

"You can count on us," Maximus replied.

It was then Faustus noticed Titus, curled up in a corner, his cheek bright red.

"Titus, are you all right, my boy?"

No response.

"Titus!"

But Titus still didn't respond. He looked at the old man, opened his mouth, tried to speak, and then gave a weak smile. Faustus turned to Maximus with a worried look.

"He hasn't said a word since he saw the body," Maximus explained. "We have tried to get him to talk but haven't had any luck."

"And his cheek? Has he hurt himself?"

"Oh, that...," Maximus mumbled, trying to avoid the question.

"He's in shock," said Septimus Demetrius. "That's not an unusual reaction. Don't worry. He'll get his voice back."

"When?" asked Faustus with concern. "His parents entrusted him to my care while they're away."

The man shrugged his shoulders. "That depends," he said. "Everyone reacts differently. Some start speaking again within the hour. For others, it takes longer. Sometimes, another shock can snap them out of it."

"I tried that...," Maximus sheepishly muttered.

"But you wanted to question him," said Faustus. "And if you've got to keep us all locked up here until everyone's answered your questions, that's no good for any of us."

Faustus bent down to the boy and shouted, "Titus!"

His tone of voice was sharp. If Titus' cheek weren't already burning, he would have been tempted to give him a slap too.

"I think I can answer for both of us," Maximus confidently suggested. "I was with Titus when we saw this man for the first time. And since then, I haven't left his side. Nor Aghiles either."

Septimus Demetrius turned to Maximus. "And you are...?"

"I'm Maximus, Titus' best friend and the son of Julius Claudius."

"Julius Claudius the senator?"

"That's right."

Septimus Demetrius gave a satisfied nod of the head. Julius Claudius was a man known by all of Rome and respected for his integrity. The mere mention of his name was a guarantee of good faith.

"Very well, your testimony will suffice," Septimus Demetrius agreed. "You told Faustus you've seen this man before."

"That's right. Yesterday, late afternoon. All three of us had spent the day tending to the animals of Titus' father while he's away..."

"All three of you?"

"Titus, Aghiles, and I."

"Aghiles?"

Maximus motioned toward his friend. "Aghiles," he said. "He's my slave."

Maximus hated to call his friend his slave, but there was no other way of putting it. His father had offered him this giant freshly arrived from Numidia for his fifteenth birthday. The two boys had quickly bonded and were now the best friends in the world. But this deep friendship still didn't cancel out the socially established master-slave relationship: Maximus held the power of life and death over Aghiles.

Septimus Demetrius shot a quick glance at Aghiles to size him up. Then he turned back to Maximus, who was, as far as Septimus was concerned, the only witness worthy of interest.

"So you saw the dead man before?" he asked.

"He called to us just as we were about to enter the house. He wanted directions to the Forum."

"Did he look nervous to you, worried?"

"Not that I can recall."

Maximus hesitated a moment, looked to Titus, and then went on. "No, I'd say he looked exhausted. When Titus was giving him directions, he staggered a little and caught hold of Titus to steady himself. He explained he was very tired."

"Was he perhaps wounded?"

Maximus widened his eyes in astonishment and answered, "I didn't think so."

"And then what? What happened next?" the investigator continued.

"Then he repeated Titus' directions and suddenly took off." Maximus stopped for a moment and added, "In the wrong direction!"

"What do you mean by that, young man?"

"He set off in the opposite direction from what Titus had just told him," Maximus said with a smile. "I can't deny that at first I thought it was precisely because of Titus' directions. They weren't exactly... Well, they weren't very clear. But Aghiles changed my mind."

"What do you mean?"

"He noticed that the man was being followed."

Septimus Demetrius flinched slightly at that. "Followed?"

"Yes, Aghiles saw someone on his heels."

"What did he look like, this man?"

Maximus shrugged his shoulders. "I don't know. It was Aghiles who saw him..."

"He was tall and strong," Aghiles interjected.

"Any other physical details?"

"Not that I remember. I only got a quick look. He was bent over the goods on the stall across the street. When the man...," Aghiles took a deep breath, "when the man who was murdered set off, he immediately raised his head and followed him."

Septimus Demetrius stared at the slave. Was he telling the truth? He seemed to be; his face was open and honest. The investigator cleared his throat before tackling the subject that interested him most.

"This man died on the doorstep of the house of Flavius Octavius," he said. "That's very surprising. Given that he was here before, it would seem that he returned on purpose. Do you have any idea what might have brought him back here?"

Maximus gave him a funny look, feigned astonishment, and, looking Septimus straight in the eye, coolly replied, "No. Not at all."

X

LOST!

"Lost? What do you mean, you lost it?"

Tiburtius stared at his feet. There was nothing he could say in his defense. He had failed to bring the goblet.

"Delitilis was our only chance of getting it back."

"I know..."

Tiburtius was filled with regret for his failure; his heart sank. He felt an awful sense of fatigue but of violent rage too. He had been so close to fulfilling his mission. He had been working on this for weeks, ever since they had learned someone had brought the goblet back to Rome. And during all this time, he had hardly slept, hardly eaten, and walked the city streets every which way, observing, asking questions, investigating.

His associates had been counting on him. If they had entrusted the mission of finding the goblet to him, it was because they knew they could rely on him. They knew he never gave up and was strong, clever, intelligent. Tiburtius had identified Delitilis, uncovered his plot, and followed him through the city. And yet, the man, and the goblet, had eluded him.

"And you have no idea where it might be?"

"No."

Tiburtius explained that he had returned to almost every place he had seen Delitilis, asking pointed questions along the way.

"It must have fallen into the hands of someone he knows," he said.

He looked at the African before him; his coppery complexion had turned almost ashen gray. His dark eyes were bloodshot, his features strained. Like Tiberius, he hadn't slept for weeks, tormented by the return of the goblet to Rome.

"Think carefully," said the African.

"I have."

"But we must not resign ourselves to the loss of that goblet," he insisted, trying to restrain his anger. "We must find it!"

Suddenly, the door flew open with a bang. A man burst into the room. Instinctively, Tiburtius shrank back against the wall into the shadows. The African slowly turned around, clenching his jaw. He had to remain calm, as natural as possible. Over time, he had learned to be surprised by nothing and to maintain a serene look in all circumstances. It was a question of self-preservation. But his heart was pounding fast.

"What is it?" he asked with only the slightest tremor in his voice.

The man who had just entered the room was unshaven and haggard. He had been running. He was breathing heavily. The African relaxed; he recognized him as one of theirs.

"You scared me," he shouted at him. "What brings you here?"

"I came as quickly as I could. As soon as I found out...," the messenger replied, swallowing hard to catch his breath.

"Why? What's happened? What have you found out?"

"Delitilis..."

"Delitilis?" repeated the African, suddenly suspicious. How could this messenger already know that Tiburtius had lost his trail? "What is it about Delitilis that seemed so urgent to you?"

"He's been found..."

"Found where?"

Itching with impatience, Tiburtius stepped out of the shadows. "So? Answer!" he demanded sharply. "He's been found? Tell us where! Quickly!"

The messenger gave a start on seeing Tiburtius; he had thought the African was alone. Then he noticed Tiburtius' drooping eyelid, his broad shoulders. He recognized him and went pale. He looked from the African to Tiburtius, then back at the African.

"Come, come! Speak up!" the latter said to him. "Where is he? It's true, Tiburtius lost his trail."

"He... he..."

"Will you please spit it out!" thundered Tiburtius.

In terror, the messenger took a slight step backward.

"Tiburtius!" said the African, trying to calm him down. "Let him speak."

The messenger opened his mouth, rolled his terrified eyes, and then stammered, "He's dead. Delitilis has been murdered!"

XI

DISCORD

"Why didn't you say anything?" Titus screeched furiously.

Unable to speak a few minutes before, Titus had now regained his voice.

"Why didn't you say anything?" he repeated, approaching Maximus with an accusing look in his eyes.

"I thought carefully about it."

"Well, I thought carefully too!" shouted Titus. "I'm going to tell them everything."

He walked with determination toward the door, but Maximus blocked his path.

"Stop, Titus! Listen to me!"

Titus stared daggers at him.

"Listen to me," Maximus repeated in a calmer voice. "I really don't think it's in our interest to talk about this goblet to anyone. In any case, not until we know what it is."

His hand still on the doorknob, Titus stopped, waiting to hear what his friend had to say.

"We have no proof it really was that man who slipped the goblet into your bag," Maximus explained. "It could have gotten in there some other way, perhaps at your father's business. There's nothing to link it to this murder yet."

"So what? If it's got nothing to do with this case, we'll at least be in the clear."

"But just think, what if the goblet really is valuable? We'll be the prime suspects."

"Suspects?" repeated Titus.

Maximus nodded. "People might think we had something to do with the murder in order to get the goblet."

"That's ridiculous! We're just kids."

"Kids they think worth interrogating like adults. The *urbaniciani* said as much to Faustus—we're all potential suspects."

Titus shivered. He didn't like this situation at all.

"And what if it's not worth anything?" Aghiles asked.

"Then it's of no interest, and there's no need to mention it," Maximus said.

"It still remains that a man was murdered," said Titus. "And I still believe that he was trying to get the goblet back."

Maximus frowned. "That's why we have to figure out where the goblet came from. Only then can we decide how to proceed."

"That's risky...," Aghiles observed, but with a glint in his eye.

Maximus said nothing, but shot his friend a look of pleasure. This case, indeed, promised to be fascinating.

But Titus sharply retorted, "I can't go along with this!"

Maximus and Aghiles looked at each other in confusion.

"I won't go along with it. You'll have to do it without me."

"Without you?" asked Maximus.

"Do what you like to figure it out, but I won't have anything to do with it. I don't want to end up strangled on someone's doorstep."

"You're over-imagining things," Maximus said with a laugh.

"And you're not imagining enough!" replied Titus in an icy tone.

"You're angry?"

"Let's just say, I'm cautious. From now on, I don't want to hear any more about that goblet. I never saw it. I don't even know what you're talking about."

Maximus smiled and asked, "So you won't say anything about it?"

"I don't know what you're talking about."

"Thank you, my friend," replied Maximus with a bow.

But Titus winced. "I have a terrible feeling you're making a big mistake."

XII

SUSPICION

The African cast a long searching look at Tiburtius, who suddenly went pale.

"It wasn't me!" he stammered. "I didn't kill him!" News of the death of Delitilis had taken him by surprise, and he was hurt by the suspicion he read in the other's eyes.

"I'd do almost anything to get that goblet back, but NOT THAT!" Tiburtius raised his voice despite himself. He couldn't let anyone think such a thing, especially after all the risks he had taken to obtain the precious object. Any suspicion of him was an insult.

The African saw how upset his companion was, distraught even. "I believe you," he said simply. "But the death of Delitilis only complicates things."

When the African and his companions learned that the goblet had returned to Rome, they at first thought it was a joke. It was impossible. For almost fifty years, it had been in safekeeping in Hispania, in a discreet place, far from greedy eyes. Its anonymity was the best guarantee of its protection.

But then things heated up. News spread that Emperor Diocletian was interested in making the goblet disappear. People said he had sent men to find it, even in Hispania, where they had recruited the services of a trusted but ruthless man, Delitilis, to destroy it.

What had driven Delitilis to disobey his orders? No one knew. Some said he had been seduced by the beauty of the goblet. But it was more likely that he suspected he could make more money—a lot of money—by selling it. Between the supporters of the emperor, who wanted it destroyed, and those who hoped to find and protect it, he no doubt thought he could easily raise the stakes.

Rumors had circulated that a man was trying to hawk a precious goblet to the highest bidder. That's how the African and his men realized that the goblet was in Rome. And from that moment, Tiburtius had been on the trail of Delitilis. And just when he was on the verge of success...

"How do you know he's been murdered?" the African questioned the messenger. "Maybe it was an accident."

Keeping a nervous eye on Tiburtius, the man shook his head and said, "He was strangled."

"Strangled?! You're sure of it?"

"Afraid so..."

"But then, if someone killed him—"

"It means he had the goblet," said Tiburtius, finishing his sentence. For he was thinking the same thing. "Someone other than us wanted to get hold of it."

"Someone ready to kill for it," added the African.

But who has the goblet now? the African wanted to know. He refused to believe all was lost. "Where was his body found?" he asked, clutching at straws.

"On the doorstep of Flavius Octavius."

That made Tiburtius shudder, and the African too, but for different reasons.

"Flavius Octavius, the wild animal trader?" they both asked at the same time, staring at the man in disbelief.

"You know Flavius Octavius?" an astonished Tiburtius asked the African, who hadn't been in Rome for very long.

"Oh... well... everyone in Rome has heard of him," he quickly replied, avoiding the question. "He sounds to me an honest man. The body of Delitilis in front of his house must just be a coincidence."

"I'm not so sure of that," Tiburtius interrupted him.

"Why not?"

"Just before I lost him, Delitilis had stopped in front of the house of Flavius Octavius. I remember it clearly. As you say, almost everyone in Rome knows who Flavius Octavius is and where he lives. His fame is enormous."

"What was Delitilis doing in front of that man's house?" the African cut him off, wishing to get to the point.

"He spoke to three boys who were just going into the house."

Tiburtius stopped a moment and searched his memory. At the time, he hadn't really paid much attention to it. But now that Delitilis had been murdered, it all took on new importance. If only he could recall a detail that would give them a new lead.

"One of the boys had a monkey on his shoulder." Tiburtius continued. "That's unusual. Delitilis spoke to him and the two others. One was very tall and black-skinned, and the other was short with brown hair, I think." Tiburtius closed his eyes, trying to visualize the scene. "No, wait, he was blond," he corrected himself. "At the time, I thought Delitilis was just trying to create a diversion or was asking for directions. But if that's where they found his body..."

The African stared at him, trying to understand what he was getting at.

"It must be because Delitilis knew those boys," he concluded.

The African remained silent. He was thinking fast. If those boys met Delitilis, there was perhaps still hope of finding the lost goblet.

"We must absolutely speak to them," he thought.

XIII

A CONSULTATION WITH A FORTUNE-TELLER

Titus walked quickly. He had urgent business at the Forum. Things had gone very wrong ever since he woke up that morning with a sneeze. He desired to know more. He wanted to know what the future, or at least the rest of the day, held for him. Only then, he believed, could he avoid any false step or bad decision. Ever since this morning, when the day started so badly, he felt overtaken by events, unable to control them. Titus wanted to take his fate back into his own hands.

From the moment Titus left the house, he was discreetly followed. Septimus Demetrius smiled with satisfaction when he saw Titus was unaccompanied. That's just what he had hoped for: to meet with the boy alone to question him. Septimus was convinced that, had he been able to talk to Titus earlier, his version of events wouldn't corroborate with that of his friend. Why was he so sure? Septimus had noticed a few glances between the two boys that spoke louder than words.

Titus stopped when he got to the Forum. As usual, the place was crowded and noisy, bustling, smelly, and disorganized. It seemed the entire city had decided to meet there at the same time. Passersby, stall vendors, street artists, pickpockets, crooks, acrobats, rich senators, women of ill repute, amateur orators—from the richest to the poorest, from the most honest citizens to the most corrupt rogues—were there this morning.

Titus carefully scanned his surroundings in the hope of spotting his man. He searched the passing crowds, looking for the familiar face. And then, suddenly, he saw the man he was seeking seated on the ground, as usual, dirty and in rags. Titus immediately approached him.

"If Maximus could see me now!" Titus thought to himself.

And, indeed, if his friend could see him, he would give him a good telling off. He never stopped telling Titus what a charlatan this man was. And yet, charlatan or not, Titus couldn't resist the temptation of consulting him.

Septimus observed Titus. What on earth was that boy doing? To his great astonishment, he went straight up to a strange old man sitting on the ground. To look at him, you would think he was a beggar with his frayed toga, worn sandals, and messy hair and beard. But Septimus could sense something behind the supposed humility of a man begging for a few crumbs. This man sat proud and upright. And he called out with liveliness to those passing by.

The fortune-teller immediately recognized Titus. With his monkey perched on his shoulder, Titus was hard to forget. It wasn't the first time the boy had come to consult him, and the old man knew he could always squeeze a few coins out of him. One look at the boy was enough for him to understand that Titus was anxious. His brow was wrinkled with worry.

"So, the day has started badly for you!" the fortune-teller called to him.

Titus stopped in his tracks. Every time, he was amazed how easily this soothsayer could read him. Titus had no doubt about the man's wisdom.

"Yes, and I'd like to know how it will continue," he replied.

The fortune-teller smiled and motioned to him to sit down next to him, though not without asking him for a fistful of sesterces first.

Septimus grinned. The boy was consulting a fortune-teller, proof that Titus wasn't totally comfortable with the events of the morning. He was surely hiding something, and Septimus was determined to find out what. Even if he had to wait. In any case, he couldn't do much else at the moment, and Titus was the only lead he had.

When Titus stood up a few minutes later, he was smiling again. The fortune-teller had told him that everything would be fine; he had only to offer up a few dried dates to his household gods, and danger would be avoided. Once he had made this offering, he could go about his business in peace.

Satisfied, Titus gave the fortune-teller a few extra sesterces to thank him for his wise advice. The man humbly thanked him as he pocketed the coins under his frayed tunic, in a purse growing heavier as the day went on. A good day, all in all, he thought. The fortune-teller watched Titus walking away. He didn't know why, but he wanted to see the boy cheer up. A few positive predictions, and the job was done.

Titus was returning home with a light heart when someone called to him from behind. He stopped, and turned around.

"Excuse me for startling you," Septimus Demetrius said to him with a friendly smile. "I saw you passing and thought you looked better. I'm delighted to see it."

A slight glint of alarm shot through Titus' eyes. He looked at the policeman and gave him a forced smile.

"Thank you," said Titus softly.

"Oh, so I see you've got your voice back."

Titus bit his lip. He shouldn't have spoken. Maybe the

policeman would have thought he was still mute. He nodded his head without saying another word.

"We're hunting the man who committed this heinous crime," Septimus went on. "When I saw you, something else occurred to me. Do you mind if I ask you a question?"

"Maximus already answered all your questions," Titus cautiously replied.

"Yes, but there's one thing I forgot to ask."

Titus swallowed hard. He didn't like the inquisitorial look of this man.

"Well, if it's really important...," he agreed.

"Thank you, Titus. It is Titus, isn't it?"

"Uh-huh."

"Perfect. Well, here it is. Do you agree with everything your friend Maximus told us?"

XIV

CONFUSION

Faustus just happened to be walking by the *vestibulum* as a slave was closing the front door. In the absence of Flavius Octavius, Faustus received all his master's visitors who came on urgent business. He would note their requests and pass them on. If there had been visitors, the slave ought to have brought them to him.

"Who was that?" he asked the slave.

"The *urbaniciani*."

"What did they want? Has there been any news?"

"I don't know. They didn't tell me."

"Then why did they come?"

"They'd been called, but they were held up on another case."

"Who called them?"

"We did."

"Someone called back the city police?" asked Faustus with astonishment.

"I don't know who. But, in any case, I told them to check with the other team."

"The other team?"

"Yes, the one that came this morning."

"What team?" insisted Faustus, growing impatient.

"The other team of *urbaniciani*. The ones that came to investigate this morning and removed the body."

"You mean the *urbaniciani* who just left weren't the same ones as this morning?"

"Oh no, these men were in uniform."

Faustus went pale. In uniform... How could he have made such a stupid mistake?

XV

RESEARCH

Aghiles heaved a sigh and yawned. "Is there much more?" he asked.

Maximus had been plunged in the library scrolls for what seemed like ages now, and Aghiles was bored to death. When Maximus had talked about carrying out an investigation, this isn't how Aghiles had imagined it. In a library? For hours? Aghiles, who didn't know how to read, was cut out for running, fighting, hunting—not for searching through scrolls in a library.

The giant Numidian looked up and down the shelves of the large room. They were filled with papyrus scrolls, thousands of them, all labeled with a little triangular tag inscribed with the title and the author's name. Normally, he would almost envy the men going through all these documents, reading them out loud, each in his own corner. But not today. He was itching for action.

"Haven't you found anything yet?"

Maximus took a moment to respond. This was painstaking research. He had started out with high hopes of finding information about famous tableware, sacred objects, or precious goblets. But whenever he thought he had found a lead, he was disappointed. There was nothing resembling the ordinary-looking goblet hidden under his tunic.

"You're not going to find anything here," Aghiles said impatiently, sweeping his eyes across the thousands of scrolls in the library. "It will take hours, and you don't even know what you're looking for."

"An agate goblet."

"Oh, well that narrows it down then," Aghiles retorted sarcastically.

It was rare for the slave to stand up to his young master like that, but his common sense told him they were wasting time.

"Have you got a better idea?" Maximus asked with annoyance.

"Let's go see the dealers. I'm sure they'll be able to tell us more than any of your books."

"Like what?"

Maximus crossed his arms with a sour look, curious to hear his slave's clever idea.

"It's provenance, where it was made," Aghiles insisted, refusing to be put off by his friend's tone. He had been thinking things over since they got to the library. He thought the dealers, of tableware in particular, could be a great help to them.

"If we knew what region this goblet came from," he said, "we could narrow down the research. And then, one of them might have heard something about this goblet, and if it's as valuable as you think."

Maximus wrinkled his nose. It annoyed him to admit it, but Aghiles was right. In any case, they were more likely to come up with leads in the marketplace than in the library—and maybe more quickly.

"All right," he reluctantly agreed. "Let's go see the dealers. But what will we tell them?"

Aghiles smiled. He had already thought of what to say. "Tell them you've broken one of your parents' goblets and want to replace it before they find out. You have no idea where they got it, and you can't ask them without having to own up to what you did."

This time, a little smile began to light up Maximus' face. Like his friend, he too was dreaming of a little action. So he rolled up the *volumen*[1] he had been reading and put it back in its little niche in the wall.

Within minutes, the two boys were taking a deep breath of fresh air in the street. They looked at each other with satisfaction and gave a nod.

"Let's go," Maximus whispered. "And let's hope your method yields better results than mine!"

Just behind the two boys, a pudgy short man hurried out of the library. He had overheard their conversation, which greatly intrigued him. Gallien—for that was his name—was a dealer, and Aghiles was right to think that the traders would be able to inform them best. He, for example, knew better than anyone the most sought-after objects on the market at the moment. And there was one in particular that every dealer wanted to get his hands on—but which so far seemed untraceable.

---

1. A book written on a papyrus scroll.

XVI

GREED

Gallien struggled to follow Maximus and Aghiles, who walked fast. He almost had to run on his stubby legs to keep up. The farther they went, the more his face flushed and the more out of breath he became. Beads of sweat rolled down his forehead, stinging his eyes and then hanging on the tip of his nose before dripping onto his generous belly.

Gallien suddenly regretted his years of overeating and drinking. He wasn't in good enough shape to keep up with these two boys. But he did have one thing in his favor: he was tenacious. When Gallien sniffed a good deal, he was like a dog with a bone—he wouldn't let it go, even if it killed him. And this time, he was sure he was on to something special. He wouldn't let them out of his sight.

Suddenly, just as they were reaching the Forum, the two boys stopped. A man stepped in front of them; he was tall and extremely muscular, with curly blonde hair. Gallien had seen him somewhere before, but he couldn't quite remember where. It would come back to him. He never forgot a face, even if he had only seen it once. That was his strong point, an advantage he had over his clients: he often knew much more about them than they knew about him.

The man and the two boys spoke for a moment together. From where he was standing, Gallien could tell the boys were hesitating, but finally they followed the man, who must have come to find them. Such a change in the game plan would have made anyone other than Gallien admit defeat. But he wasn't one to give up. His main goal was to connect these two boys to some place or some person so as to identify them. Once he had done that, it would be easy to catch up with them and find out more about this goblet they had been talking about.

He continued to follow them, and fortunately for him, the meeting with this man had slowed down the boys' pace. It was easier to keep up with them, and Gallien wasn't quite so out of breath.

They sped up, though, at a street corner. When Gallien arrived at the street the three had turned down, there was no one there. The trio had disappeared. Gone! The little street was dark and empty. There wasn't a sound. Gallien could hardly believe it. He retraced his steps, looking all around him. There was no sign of the little group anywhere. He scanned the crowd, returned several yards down the alleyway, and then retraced his steps. He looked in every direction, hurrying on in the hope of spotting them. But the man and the boys he did not see.

Gallien exploded with a curse. He could kick himself for not approaching the boys as soon as he had overheard them in the library. After all, there would have been nothing odd about him eavesdropping on their conversation. He could then have supplied them with information. Instead, he had decided to follow them.

But Gallien wasn't ready to give up the chase. He still couldn't remember the name of that well-built, blonde man who had stopped to talk to the boys, but he knew he was someone important. Maybe even someone close to the emperor. In any case, he had a vague feeling that the man's arrival there wasn't a coincidence, which only confirmed for Gallien that he was on the trail of a juicy deal. Very juicy, if his instincts were correct.

Gallien decided to go back down the side street. Those three couldn't have just disappeared into thin air. They must have slipped down an alleyway he hadn't noticed or entered a villa and found some other way out.

The little man went sniffing down the tiniest of alleyways—examining every corner with care, trying every doorknob, and listening for any sound, but there were no signs of life anywhere. One house had two windows facing the alley, but they were too high for anyone to reach from the ground. The two boys and their blonde companion must have disappeared behind these doorways—but which one?

Gallien decided to have one last go. He went back to the first door and knocked. "Is anyone there?" he called.

He strained his ear and waited, but no one answered. He knocked at the second door. Still nothing. No one opened it. He couldn't hear the slightest movement. Both buildings seemed to be vacant.

Gallien then decided to go around the corner. Maybe he would find exits there and figure out how they could have gotten away. When Gallien returned to the main street, he looked up and saw the wall of the Colosseum rising above him not far away. He hadn't paid much attention to it earlier. Then, like a thunderbolt, it came back to him. Septimus! Yes, that was the name of the man who had approached the boys. Septimus, the famous gladiator!

XVII

PRISONERS!

A faint voice reached Maximus through the deep fog engulfing him.

"Is anyone there?" the voice called again.

It had hardly been audible, but it was enough to pierce the haze and bring him slowly back to consciousness. Then a door opened. Something landed with a thud. There was a groan, then the rattling of a key in a lock. The noises sounded far away, disappeared, and then gave way to thick silence.

When Maximus fully regained consciousness, he grimaced and raised his hand to his head. There was a terrible throbbing in his skull, like loud, painful hammer blows. He cautiously opened one eye, but a violent stab at the back of his head forced him to close it again. Maximus took a deep breath and tried to understand what was happening to him and where he was. But it was all a blur. He struggled to gather his wits. He recalled a corpse, Titus, the library, a goblet... At the thought of that, he suddenly opened both eyes, which caused another shooting pain. The goblet! Now it all came back to him. Where was it? He patted all over his tunic, hoping to find a bulge, but there was nothing under its folds.

Little by little, Maximus pieced together the events of the last few hours. He remembered the body in front of Titus' house. Then the disagreement with his friend. His research in the library with Aghiles. Their meeting with Septimus Demetrius, the head of the local police. His request that they follow him to answer a few further questions regarding his investigation. His hesitation to begin with. Then, the blow to his head. After that, everything was a blank.

Maximus searched the darkness around him. He could hardly see a thing. There was just one sliver of light coming from a little opening at the top of the wall. Not enough to see what this room was or what was in it. But he could just make out a dark form lying on the ground about a yard away from him. It must be Aghiles. He called to his friend.

"Aghiles!" he whispered, worried about drawing anyone's attention.

The dark form close to him moved slightly, but a response came from the other side of the room.

"Maximus?"

Maximus stiffened. "Titus?" he asked.

"Maximus! You're here!"

Titus rose in a flash. He rushed in the darkness to his friend and almost fell upon him.

"You're here!" he repeated. "By Jupiter, you're here!"

Titus ran his hands over Maximus' head, trying to reassure himself he was really there. He felt his shoulders, his nose, his hair...

"Ow! Watch out!" Maximus shouted as his friend touched the lump on the back of his head.

"I'm sorry. So sorry. If you knew how happy I am to see you! I thought I'd never see you again!"

"What are you doing here?"

"Septimus Demetrius came to talk to me. I thought he was from the police."

"That makes two of us."

"Oh no, oh no! What are we going to do now?"

"Were you here when they..." Maximus searched for the right word to describe it. "When they brought us here?"

"No, they held me somewhere else, for hours, I think. They only transferred me to this dungeon a few minutes ago," Titus replied.

"When they locked the door, I thought I was going to die. I thought I was all alone. Except for the rats..." Titus shivered. "What a horrible thought!"

At that moment, a little groan made them turn to the form lying on the ground.

"Aghiles?" Maximus called.

"Owwww," groaned his slave as he slowly sat up, rubbing his head. "I feel like I've been stampeded by a herd of elephants."

He squinted his eyes, trying to distinguish the form of his two friends in the darkness.

"Titus!?" he said with astonishment. "What are you doing here?!"

"It's Septimus Demetrius," came Maximus' somber reply.

Aghiles gave another groan. How could he not have seen it coming?

"What are we going to do now?" asked Titus.

Maximus really had no idea. And the throbbing in his head kept him from thinking clearly.

Beside him, Titus heaved a great sigh. "And to think the fortune-teller promised me the day would get better!"

Maximus winced at the annoying reference to that conman. But this wasn't the time to argue with his friend. They had to remain united if they wanted to get out of this mess.

"And the goblet?" Aghiles suddenly asked.

"Gone," said Maximus. "At least we were right about that: it's the key to this whole affair." A light went on in Maximus' head. He turned to Titus and asked, "Septimus Demetrius, how did he know? Did you tell him I had the goblet?"

Titus went bright red and inwardly thanked the gods for keeping his friends from realizing the truth. "No, no, of course not! I told you, I don't know anything about that goblet," he replied.

"But if you didn't say anything, what are Aghiles and I doing here? And why has the goblet disappeared?"

"I really couldn't say," Titus assured him. "Maybe Septimus Demetrius had you frisked."

Maximus returned to the attack. "Are you sure you didn't say anything?"

"No... I mean, yes... I'm sure."

"Not even a tiny little bit?"

"Not even a bit."

"Nothing at all?"

"No, really..."

"Maybe just a little detail..."

"No."

Titus' answers were less and less assured. Maximus kept at him. He knew his friend; he knew he wasn't brave. It wouldn't take much to break him, given a muscular interrogation. Given *any* interrogation, for that matter. "You didn't perhaps hint at something?"

"I don't think so?" Titus whistled in the air.

"You don't think so, or you're sure?"

"It's just... it's just... he threatened to break my little finger," Titus stammered. "I only told him you maybe might have taken it."

Maximus gave a weary look and raised an eyebrow.

"And that you were going to the library," Titus went on.

"I don't suppose you gave him my address, while you were at it," Maximus retorted with more than a little sarcasm.

"Maybe... I don't know anymore..."

Maximus threw himself at Titus. He wanted to punch him. Aghiles held him back. "Maximus, no!" he said. "Hurting your friend will do us no good."

"And just think of poor Dux who must be looking for me everywhere," Titus moaned, trying to change the subject.

Maximus sat bolt upright. "Dux isn't with you?" he asked.

"No, they put him out as soon as I realized Septimus Demetrius wasn't who he said he was."

"So Dux knows where you are?" Maximus' voice trembled with renewed hope.

"He's only a monkey," Aghiles intervened.

Maximus smiled. "Maybe, but he's our only hope."

XVIII

A NEW VISITOR

"There's a man asking to see Flavius Octavius," a slave announced to Faustus.

"And did you tell him he's away? That I'm the only one here?"

"Yes, but he insists that someone receive him. Titus perhaps. He knows him. He claims it's urgent."

"Well then, show him to Titus."

"He's not here."

Faustus raised a quizzical eyebrow. "Not here?"

"He went to the Forum to consult his fortune-teller and hasn't come back since."

The old man stiffened. When his master was away, what he hated most was having to deal with Titus. That boy was unpredictable, swinging between highs and lows. He took full advantage of the freedom Flavius Octavius had always allowed his son. Too much freedom for Faustus' liking; he would prefer to keep the boy on a tighter leash during his parents' absence.

"Are Maximus and Aghiles here?" he asked, on the alert for trouble.

"They're out as well."

Faustus relaxed. If the three boys were together, nothing could happen to his master's son.

"There's no need to wait for Titus," he said in a calm voice. "Who knows what time he'll get home."

"What about the visitor?" asked the slave. "What should I do about him?"

"Bring him to me. If it's as urgent as he says, perhaps I can help him."

When the slave showed the visitor into the room, Faustus could hardly hide his surprise. He was expecting a Roman, not a man with coppery skin and crinkly hair. This man, clearly a North African, had all the air of a slave, yet he advanced without hesitation to greet Faustus with assurance. Faustus stared at him, trying to remember where he might have seen him before. But he had to admit, his face didn't really ring a bell.

"And you are...?" he asked.

The African considered a moment before answering. Better to give a false name.

"I'm Gratus," he finally replied.

Faustus pinched his lips. That name didn't mean anything to him either.

"I'm told you wished to see my master or his son on urgent business. They are not in, but perhaps I can help you."

The African wrinkled his nose. "Do you know when Titus will be back?" he asked. "I wished to offer him my condolences."

Faustus suddenly went white. "Your condolences? Has someone died without my being informed?"

"I heard that you'd lost a friend. This morning." The African was careful not to reveal too many details.

"This morning? But..."

"People are saying... they're saying there's been a murder. How horrible. Titus must be deeply upset."

Faustus narrowed his eyes and looked his visitor up and down. He was again on his guard, suspicious of this stranger. He met a few too many people who were interested in this murder. The old man didn't know why, but this didn't bode well. If only Titus were home, he would feel reassured. His instincts told him it wasn't good for the boy to be out.

"Oh, the corpse from this morning!" Faustus exclaimed with an unconcerned air. "That was nothing."

"But a man is dead, all the same!" the African indignantly retorted.

"Of course; that's not what I meant. But he was a perfect stranger. Titus doesn't know who he could be."

"I hope not," replied the African, continuing this game of cat and mouse. "I was told it was someone close to Titus and imagined the shock it must have been for him."

The two men fell silent and stared at each other. Neither was duped by this charade they were playing. Faustus was convinced this man before him had come to dig for information about the dead man. For his part, the African had noted Faustus' reserve.

Within minutes, the African left the house of Flavius Octavius. Faustus summoned one of the house's most trusted slaves and said, "Follow the man who's just left. I want to know what he's hiding and why he came here."

XIX

DUX

Gallien hurried away out of the little side street. Now that he had identified the man who had spoken to the two boys, he had no intention of hanging around. He knew Septimus by reputation and had no wish to cross his path. There clearly was some funny business going on here, but if Gallien got too involved in it, Septimus would be after him as well.

Having been one of the most celebrated gladiators of his generation, Septimus had won not only his freedom, but the trust of the emperor as well. The emperor had taken notice of his bravery in the circus games. But he also admired the cool nerve Septimus showed when it was a question of finishing off his adversary; for, indeed, Septimus never showed any mercy and never asked for any from the gladiators he fought. The emperor needed a man like him to carry out his most unsavory commands, to handle his most delicate business, or to resolve his most secret disputes. Septimus went directly from his gladiatorial career to the emperor's service. And no one who knew his reputation dared cross him.

Gallien had only moved a few hundred yards away when he felt something strike his back. He cried out. Fingers were gripping his shoulder. He closed his eyes, preparing himself for the worst. Septimus... it could only be Septimus who had grabbed him. Gallien trembled from head to foot. He had met his final hour, of that he was sure. Septimus must suspect him of being in cahoots with those boys.

"But I haven't... I haven't...," he stammered.

His forehead was dripping with a cold, clammy sweat. His legs turned to jelly. He wanted to call out, to shout to the crowd to help him, but the people went merrily on their way without realizing what was happening to him, that he was about to die. The few who did look toward him simply looked amused. He was about to die, and all the onlookers could do was laugh.

Gallien swallowed hard, closed his eyes, and called on the gods to come to his help. Jupiter! Mars! Vulcan! And why not Bacchus too! It made no difference to him, as long as one of them came to his rescue. Gallien had never been very religious, but now he swore before all the Roman gods that he would make lavish offerings to all of them if only he got out of this alive.

And then a tiny hand gave a tug on his ear. Gallien opened his eyes in astonishment. This was a strange divine intervention. But then he felt another tug on his ear, followed by fingers pulling his hair.

"Owww!" moaned Gallien. Someone had just pulled out a tuft of his hair. Gallien turned his head, and let out a cry. "A monkey!"

Yes, it was a monkey sitting on his shoulder, pulling his hair, his ears, and now his nose as well. And it was letting out plaintive little squeaks.

"Oh, you filthy little beast!" Gallien, having calmed down, brushed his shoulder. "Get off of me!"

Off balance, the little animal slipped backward, grabbed hold of Gallien's clothing, steadied itself, and jumped to the ground.

But no sooner had its paws hit the ground than it scurried back up and perched itself back on his shoulder.

"Will you leave me alone!?" Gallien thundered. He grabbed the animal by the scruff of the neck and threw it as far as he could.

But the monkey was agile. It simply did a little somersault and returned to the charge. Back on Gallien's shoulder, he again tugged at his clothes and his hair.

"Argh! You beast! Let go of me!"

But the animal only held on all the tighter. Gallien shook himself, and started a funny little dance, hopping about every which way, but nothing worked. The animal refused to loosen its grip. Gallien couldn't get rid of it. Now the crowd, indifferently passing by, began slowing down to stop and look. When Gallien tried to swat the animal off his shoulder, a disapproving murmur rose among the people. Gallien gave an apologetic look and sadly bowed his head.

"Sorry, I'm sorry. This is my monkey," he added with a forced chuckle. "We often play like this."

The monkey, who seemed to understand what this little man had just said, immediately perched right on the top of his head and gave a big toothy smile. A child applauded. One man laughed, and then another.

So Gallien, looking ridiculous, bowed to the crowd like an actor, took the monkey in his arms, and moved slowly away. When he got to a quieter little place, he squeezed the animal tight and threatened it.

"Okay, now you're going to leave me alone."

But the animal gave him an offended look, wriggled out of Gallien's grip, climbed back up onto his head, and started pulling his hair again. The animal's persistence was equal to Gallien's annoyance.

What Gallien didn't know was that Dux—for it was Dux all right—was without doubt the most stubborn monkey in the city. There was nothing very remarkable about that, since there weren't that many monkeys in Rome. But Dux was nonetheless particularly stubborn and mischievous. Titus knew that only too well since even he couldn't always make Dux obey him.

Flavius Octavius had given Dux to his son as a present. When he received him last year for his thirteenth birthday, he immediately named him Dux, which means "general." Titus thought it would be highly amusing to be able to give orders to a high-ranking army officer. But the fact was, Titus never quite managed it; and, of the two of them, it was Dux who gave the orders. So there was no doubt that in this battle of wills between Gallien and the monkey, it was the animal who would win.

And that's just what happened. Having tried threats, cajoling, intimidation, force, and scorn, Gallien still couldn't get rid of the monkey, which went on pulling at him as though trying to make him retrace his steps. After what seemed an eternity, Gallien finally gave in. "If that's the only way to get rid of this animal...," he thought to himself.

From pulling funny faces to slaps with his paws, from hair-pulling to ear-pinching, Dux managed to get Gallien to go back. But when they arrived at the turn into the little side street, the merchant stiffened.

"Oh, no, not there!" he shouted categorically.

The animal's antics had made him forget his worries about Septimus, but now that he was back before this little side street, they all came flooding back.

The little monkey hopped all the more on his shoulder.

"You're not getting me to go down there," Gallien grumbled.

Dux clung to his neck and mimicked a tragic look.

"And don't try to soften me up."

The monkey hugged his cheek to Gallien's.

"No, that won't work with me," Gallien insisted, forgetting he was actually talking to a monkey. "I won't take one step further."

As he was speaking, Gallien felt the animal suddenly tense.

"What? What? What is it?"

Dux jumped to the ground, ran to a wall, and then returned to Gallien, tugging at the edge of his tunic. Then Dux went back to the wall, ran to Gallien, and back again to the wall. While the monkey was distracted, Gallien considered quietly slipping out of sight. But that was without counting on Dux, who latched onto him and pulled him all the more.

"Okay! All right! Calm down!"

The little monkey stopped. And it was then that Gallien heard it. A long whistling.

XX

CONTACT

"He won't come!"

Titus hung his head in despair. He rubbed his stiff, aching neck and stretched. He had been whistling up toward the tiny opening at the top of the wall. He could hardly see any daylight, and it was impossible for the three friends to know what was on the other side. But it was the only contact they had with the outside world.

"Keep whistling!"

Maximus tried to sound upbeat, but he too felt his courage draining away. He and Aghiles had searched every inch of the room where they were imprisoned for a way of escape. To start with, there was the door: it was very solid, hard wood. They had banged on the door and called for help for a long time, but there was no response. They were sunk in such total silence, they wondered if they had been locked up and simply forgotten. After all, their kidnappers had gotten what they wanted: the goblet.

Aghiles had rammed his shoulder against the door, trying to break it off its hinges, but without success. And now his shoulder was aching. The two boys had felt along the walls with their fingertips, searching for a crack or a loose stone that could help them discover some way out. But all they could feel was the damp chill of the walls and moss in some places.

Titus started whistling again, without much hope, when suddenly, for just a second, he seemed to see a shadow block the light from the little window. He gave another whistle. The shadow hopped about, disappeared, and then returned. Titus could hear his heart thumping in his chest. He whistled even louder and gave a few trills. Maximus and Aghiles immediately noticed the change in their friend's tone and approached him.

"Did you see something?" Maximus asked in a low voice. Then he too saw the same shadow moving across the thin ray of light. He smiled.

"Dux!" Titus called quietly. "Dux, is that you?"

They could just make out a little squeak.

Titus turned to Maximus and Aghiles with an air of triumph. "It's Dux!" he exclaimed. He stretched toward the little window and said, "Dux, you've got to get us out of here!"

The animal gave another squeak before disappearing.

The three boys strained their ears. They thought they could hear muffled grumblings, but they couldn't be sure. Their dungeon was so well hidden underground, they could hardly hear outside noises.

"Dux!" Titus called all the louder. "Come here, Dux!" He gave a long whistle. Within a few seconds, a bigger, fatter shadow appeared, blocking all the light. Titus gulped. He was frightened. He didn't know what to do. Behind him, Maximus and Aghiles were just as worried.

"Psst!" they heard.

The three boys trembled and raised their heads to the window.

"Psst! Is anyone there?"

"Yes!" moaned Titus, overcome with emotion. "Yes, we're being held prisoner. Please help us!"

There was a long silence. Titus bit his lip.

Maximus cleared his throat and hopefully asked, "Who are you?"

Still no response. Then, worse, the shadow moved slightly away. But a stifled cry reached their ears.

"Oh, you blasted animal!"

Maximus couldn't help smiling as he imagined Dux attacking this stranger.

At last, the shadow returned, larger than ever.

"Where's Septimus?" the stranger worriedly asked.

Maximus looked to Aghiles, then to Titus. Septimus? How did this man know who had abducted them? Could this be one of the fake policeman's henchmen who had a change of heart and wanted to help them?

"He's not here. He locked us up and left us here," Maximus replied.

He had no idea if what he said was true, but it seemed their only chance of help. If Septimus were still around, they would just have to deal with it.

The stranger clearly didn't know what to think. After a long pause, he asked, "Do you have it?"

The boys exchanged puzzled looks.

"Have what?"

"The goblet."

Maximus could hardly hide his surprise. He tried to reply as calmly as possible.

"Yes. We have. Or at least, it's in a safe place. If you set us free, it's yours. We don't want to hear another word about that cursed object!"

"What? But...," Titus whispered.

"Okay," the stranger replied. And from the tone of his voice, they could tell he was smiling. "I'll help you."

XXI

TO THE RESCUE!

"This is madness, total madness!" Gallien went on grumbling.

He was doing his best to look natural but couldn't help looking over his shoulder to make sure no one was following him. He looked to the right, to the left, behind him, scanning the crowd with a worried eye. Even the least observant passerby would immediately suspect him of being up to something. But Gallien got lucky: no one took any notice of him.

Gallien walked stiffly, limping with every step, as though one of his legs simply refused to bend. In fact, he was hiding a long iron bar beneath his cloak. He had it clutched tight to his thigh for fear of dropping it. It was a good thing Maximus, Aghiles, and Titus couldn't see him, or they would lose all hope. As far as discretion went, you couldn't imagine a worse co-conspirator.

The iron bar had been Maximus' idea. It was the only thing that could be slipped through the tiny opening at the top of the wall. And then, with any luck, they could use it to pry open the door.

Just a few yards away, the boys were starting to get impatient.

"He's not coming back," insisted Titus, ever the pessimist.

"Stop saying that," grumbled Maximus. "He won't pass up an opportunity like this."

"What opportunity?"

"The goblet, of course. He clearly wants it. I don't know where it comes from or whom it belongs to, but it's obviously priceless."

"But how could he have known about the goblet?" Aghiles asked with astonishment.

"Well, I grant you, that's a bit of a mystery. Maybe he's in partnership with Septimus but decided to take what he can for himself."

"Yes, but may I remind you, we don't *have* that goblet!" Titus bitterly retorted. "You told that man we had it, but that's not true."

"So what? He doesn't know that. All that matters is that he *thinks* we have it."

"And then what?"

"And then, we'll consider our options."

"But what will we do if he's big and strong and decides to take vengeance and rip us to shreds?"

Knowing his friend's doubtful courage, Maximus smiled. "Well then, I'd still rather be ripped to shreds than rot away in here."

A shiver ran down Titus' spine as he thought of all the little beasties that might visit them as soon as night fell. He sighed. They simply had to trust this unknown man and pray to the gods that he wasn't built like Hercules.

Suddenly, a scraping against the wall made all three boys jump. Aghiles was the first to spot the iron bar being lowered down through the little window.

Aghiles caught hold of the bar and weighed it in his hands. It wasn't very heavy but ought to do the trick.

Maximus looked up and called toward the window, "That's perfect, thanks! Wait for us outside. We're on our way." Then, turning to Aghiles, he whispered, "It's up to you now, my friend."

The three boys groped their way to the other end of the room. They explored the door with their fingertips, searching for somewhere to slip in the iron bar and pry the door off its hinges. In the end, they decided the middle of the door might be the easiest to break apart.

"I've got it!" Aghiles suddenly shouted. He had found a chink between the planks of wood.

He slipped the iron bar into the gap. It was just at the right height, at waist level, where he could use the full weight of his powerful body.

Once he had planted the bar solidly in the crack, Aghiles grabbed it with both hands and pushed it with all his strength and a great "oof!" The wood gave a loud creak; its panels buckled but remained intact. The bar slid down the gap, throwing Aghiles on his back along with it. But the giant Numidian got back up, grabbed the bar, stuck it back in the door, and began all over again. The wood was very thick. It was clear he would need to have several goes at it.

But after a dozen attempts, the two planks of the door had hardly budged. Feeling with their fingertips, they could hardly tell the difference.

"Ok, what if we help you?" suggested Maximus.

With that, all three boys grabbed hold of the bar and, at Aghiles' signal, gave one great pull. The wood creaked, cracked a bit, and then the iron bar snapped in two, throwing all three friends flat on their backs.

"No, no, no!" Maximus shouted in exasperation, throwing the useless bit of metal clanging to the ground.

Aghiles tried to use the remaining piece of metal stuck in the door as a lever. But it was now too small to grasp.

"Maybe if you use it like a chisel," suggested Titus, whose panic was rising as their chances faded.

That didn't sound like a bad idea. So Aghiles pulled out the piece of iron still stuck in the door and gave a good look at its broken edge. It was razor-sharp. Then, very carefully, he began working away at the wood where it had started to pull away. Maximus grabbed the other end of iron he had thrown aside and gave him a hand with all his might.

In the alleyway outside, Gallien was growing impatient. The escape was taking too long, and he feared discovery.

"How's it going?" he shouted into the cellar. All he heard was a muffled groan.

Gallien straightened up and rubbed his neck, stiff with stretching forward to hear what was happening. He was just about to step away and stretch his legs when Dux started to become excited.

"What's up with you?"

In answer, Dux began nervously hopping around him. Just as Gallien was about to brush him off, he heard footsteps coming down the alleyway. Terrified, Gallien flattened himself against the wall, praying the darkness would hide him. For indeed, a man was hurrying toward him.

Gallien held his breath. All he could hear was his racing heartbeat and the boys' furious banging on the door. The noise echoed through the alleyway. Till then, Gallien hadn't realized just how much noise they had been making. The man who had entered the alley immediately heard the pounding as well. He rushed to the first doorway he came to, the one just a few yards away from the petrified Gallien, and disappeared inside in fright as fast as he could.

XXII

SECOND THOUGHTS

Since he had taken the goblet from Maximus, Septimus had been considering what to do. While he had been hunting for it, the matter had seemed very simple. All he had to do was find it and take it immediately to Emperor Diocletian, as he had been ordered. But now that he had this highly coveted object in his hands, Septimus wasn't so sure anymore. Just like Delitilis a few months earlier, he was having second thoughts.

When Septimus discovered the goblet hidden under Maximus' cloak, his reaction had been the same as that of Delitilis—disappointment. He couldn't understand how such an apparently insignificant object could arouse such passions. He had expected something totally different.

Septimus had been told that the goblet was simple, but still he had imagined that at least it would have been made from a precious metal, like gold or silver. He thought it would be a priceless treasure worth thousands of sesterces. But the goblet was nothing of the kind. True, agate wasn't a stone commonly used in Rome, but the stone alone wasn't enough to give the goblet great value.

Ordinarily, Septimus wasn't a man to dither. His long career as a gladiator had taught him that the slightest hesitation could prove fatal, that it's best to strike first and ask questions later. And he wasn't greedy either. The lure of gain had never motivated him. He preferred action to money, danger to an easy life. And, in the end, Septimus trusted only in himself. The gods had never been of any help to him. He prayed to no divinity; he feared no supernatural power. For him, things were either concrete, real, and tangible or they were nothing at all.

There was nothing then to keep Septimus from simply carrying out his orders. And yet, doubts nagged at him. Though he couldn't quite put his finger on it, something was making him hesitate.

As Septimus turned this strange feeling over and over in his mind, a noise made him raise his head. There was a sinister creaking noise coming from below.

XXIII

RUN FOR YOUR LIFE!

The hinges at last gave way! As Aghiles rushed at the door with his shoulder, it suddenly broke open, sending the giant Numidian crashing forward, taking the man coming toward him down with him. Before the man had time to get up, Aghiles gave him a walloping punch in the jaw, sending him sprawling backwards. The man slammed his head against the wall, passed out, and collapsed.

"All clear!" Aghiles shouted, rubbing his knuckles. He hadn't spared their jailer the full force of his strength. He wasn't likely to come around any time soon.

Maximus rushed out of their prison with Titus at his heels. There was a stairway in front of them, the only way out. Aghiles rushed up it.

"Come on, hurry up!" he shouted. The noise they had made would have put everyone on the alert.

The stairway led up to a long corridor. Which way? Right? Left? Aghiles gave Maximus a questioning look. Maximus nodded to the right. Unless he was mistaken, that was where the street ought to be. But as they went to the right, footsteps coming toward them made them turn back.

"This way," whispered Maximus, doing an about-turn.

The boys ran fast. They could hear hurried footsteps behind them.

"Hey!"

A shout behind them made them jump. The man chasing them had also just entered the corridor. Maximus, Titus, and Aghiles ran even faster. They came out into an atrium. Several rooms were attached to this interior courtyard, but at first glance it was impossible to tell which one would have an exit to the street.

Maximus rushed to the first room. It was small and poorly lit—with no exit. He came back out and shook his head at his two friends.

"Go on," Aghiles whispered under his breath. Looking behind him, he added, "I'll take care of him."

Aghiles flattened himself against the wall at the end of the corridor. He clenched his fists, ready to strike. In the meantime, Titus and Maximus explored the next room.

When Septimus arrived in the atrium, he was met with a terrible blow to his forehead. The shock and surprise took his breath away, but his confusion was short-lived. He immediately gathered his wits and fought back with a right hook to Aghiles' side. Maximus' slave doubled over and then rushed head-on at his foe. He struck Septimus in the stomach and grabbed him by the waist to throw him off balance. But Septimus dislocated Aghiles' jaw with his knee. Aghiles collapsed in pain. Septimus took advantage to jump on Aghiles and shower him with blows. Aghiles still found the strength to give Septimus a good kick in the stomach.

The former gladiator took the blow with a half smile. His opponent was tougher than he thought. He liked that. Staggering, Aghiles struggled to his feet. Through his swollen eyelids, he could see Maximus and Titus running to yet another room. He had to hold out, whatever the cost, to allow them time to escape. Stunned, the giant Numidian gathered his strength, stumbled against a pillar and collapsed to the ground.

"Aghiles!!!" he could hear his friends yelling before he lost consciousness. Maximus seemed to have found the way out.

With his opponent knocked out, Septimus turned his attention to Titus and Maximus and rushed to stop them. With one hand, he grabbed Titus by the collar. Titus struggled and kicked furiously without ever landing a blow on Septimus, who suddenly let him go. Titus went sprawling down against a chest. In the meantime, Maximus had opened the street door, but Septimus caught him as well. Wringing his neck, he dragged him back inside.

"What a shame," he said between gritted teeth. "If only you'd behaved yourself in the cellar, you'd have been fine. I'd have brought the goblet to the emperor, freed you the next day, and then disappeared. It was all so simple. But now? Hmm..."

As he was speaking, Septimus realized that what he just described was what he should have done in the first place. Enough of this soul-searching. He needed to bring Diocletian what he had demanded.

Maximus grabbed Septimus' arm. The man was strangling him. Maximus scratched him, dug his fingernails into his skin, trying to undo his hold on him. His eyes were bulging; he was beginning to gasp for breath. He felt his blood beating ever louder in his temple.

Suddenly, Septimus relaxed his grip. Aghiles had somehow gotten back on his feet and, from behind, kicked Septimus to the ground. Now it was the gladiator who was flat on his back. Aghiles jumped him. Next to him, Maximus was rubbing his neck, trying to breathe. As for Titus, he was still lying half-stunned, slumped on the floor next to the chest.

Aghiles and Septimus rolled on the floor, fists and knees flying. Aghiles was now in a fury. He hit, bit, and struggled like a devil. At first taken by surprise, Septimus now began to get the upper hand. He let rip another blow to Aghiles' nose. A bone cracked. Blood spurted all over. Septimus immobilized Aghiles, straddling his chest with all his weight. Aghiles struggled to get free, but the gladiator was too heavy. Septimus raised his fist and made a furious growl. Then, to Aghiles' immense surprise, Septimus collapsed on top of him, like a dead weight.

XXIV

OUT OF ACTION

The statuette still in his hands, Gallien looked from Septimus to Aghiles then back again. He couldn't believe what he had just done. And, suddenly, he began to giggle. A nervous, almost hysterical giggle.

"I did it!" he rejoiced. "I killed him. I killed Septimus."

Then, suddenly, Gallien turned white. He rushed to Septimus and shook him.

"By Jupiter, I've killed him," he stammered.

Gallien went from excitement to sheer panic. He was completely out of his league. When he had seen the door open a few minutes earlier and heard the noise of a fight, he had approached very cautiously. Then, when he saw Septimus hitting one of the two boys he had spotted in the library, he didn't stop to think. He grabbed the statuette and struck the ex-gladiator on the head with it. And now, Septimus was dead. Surely, the emperor would hunt Gallien down, condemn him to death, perhaps even deliver him to the lions.

"What have I done? What will he do to me?" he moaned.

"Not much, if you've actually killed him," Maximus dryly remarked.

Aghiles sat up with a groan.

"Thank you," he said gravely to Gallien. "You arrived in the nick of time."

Another moan made them both turn their heads. Gallien looked toward Titus in confusion.

"But...," spluttered Gallien, "but I thought there were only two of you!"

"Titus joined us... a little later," croaked Maximus, still feeling the effects of Septimus' hands around his throat.

At just that moment, Dux skipped into the room and jumped on Titus' shoulder, giggling with joy.

"Ah, go on, Dux. Dux, stop it!" Titus repeated, now perfectly back to his senses.

Gallien then leaned over Septimus, still unmoving in the middle of the room.

"Do you think I've really killed him?" he asked fretfully.

Maximus leaned over him too and shook him. "No, he's still breathing. But it's better for us if we're not here when he comes around."

Gallien was petrified. "He's not dead?" he stammered. "But then he'll want to take revenge."

A noise in the atrium drew their attention. Maximus turned to look. The man he had knocked out on leaving the cellar had just entered the interior courtyard.

"I think it's time we made our exit," he whispered, "before he spots us."

He leaned once again over Septimus, stood up, and then signaled to the three others to follow him. But as he was going through the door, the man spotted him.

"Hey! You there!" he shouted, setting after them in hot pursuit.

XXV

A DISCREET MISSION

The slave Faustus sent to follow the African hadn't expected
the chase to be so complicated. The African had only been a
few yards ahead of him, but he kept doubling back and making
unexpected detours. He would enter a shop, exit by the back
door, enter an alleyway, and then retrace his steps, leading him
around in circles. Either he didn't know where he was going,
or he was trying to cover his tracks. The slave thought the latter
was the more likely.

At last, the African entered a house. The slave kept watch
from a discreet distance a few yards away from the door, waiting
for him to come out again. But the minutes went by without
the African re-emerging. Clearly this was the man's address.
Faustus would be pleased.

When he got back to his master's house, the slave immediately gave Faustus a detailed report of his mission. The old man
was indeed pleased. He knew he could trust this man.

"Perfect," Faustus replied. Too many strange things had been
going on since the start of that day for him to do nothing.
"I need to get to the bottom of this business before Flavius
Octavius returns. I'll warn the *urbaniciani* and have them take
a look at this man's house."

XXVI

AT THE BARBERSHOP

Titus, Maximus, Aghiles, and Gallien ran from the house. Dux hardly had time to leap onto his master's shoulder. They immediately turned down the alleyway leading back to the main street. They had to melt into the crowd. That was their only chance of outdistancing their pursuer. Fortunately, the many passersby were all on their way toward the Colosseum.

"This way!" Maximus cried, nodding toward the Forum.

He cast a quick look behind him and saw the man pursuing them up the street. He was alone and would quickly catch up with them. Of course, he wouldn't be able to do much to them, surrounded by the crowd like this, but he could call for help or alert nearby soldiers.

"Let's split up," said Maximus. "We'll have a better chance of losing him. Meet up back at my place."

There was no need for long explanations. In an instant, they had separated and lost themselves in the crowd, each one headed in a different direction.

"Where are you going?" screamed Gallien, still rooted to the spot in the middle of the street.

The man following them looked in his direction but didn't recognize him; he had caught only a fleeting glimpse of him earlier. The man searched the crowd. At the same moment, Maximus was seized with remorse at having abandoned the man who had probably saved his life. He retraced his steps and grabbed Gallien by the sleeve. The man trailing them spotted this and recognized Maximus. He set off at a run in their direction.

"Couldn't you keep your mouth shut!" Maximus berated Gallien under his breath. "Run!"

Gallien followed close on Maximus' heels but couldn't keep up with him. At the risk of capture, Maximus slowed his pace.

"Come on! Faster!" Maximus urged him on.

Gallien was trotting along on his little legs more than running. It was only a matter of seconds before he and Maximus would be caught by this man whose way, luckily for them, was obstructed by the crowds. For a moment, Maximus considered leaving Gallien behind, but he thought better of it and dragged him into a barber shop. He grabbed one of the wigs on display, stuck it on his all-too-recognizable blond hair, and forcibly sat Gallien down on a stool.

"Well! Don't mind me!" the shopkeeper exclaimed. "Just help yourself, why don't you!"

Maximus stared him down. "You're talking to a very rich man," he warned him, pointing to Gallien.

With that, he grabbed tweezers from a table and tweaked a gray hair from the little man's head.

"Ouch! That hurt!" shouted Gallien.

"Keep quiet!" Maximus hissed.

The man following them had stopped at the shop door.

Maximus leaned further over Gallien's head. The little man had now gone red. One after another, Maximus plucked his gray hairs, imitating the gestures of the barber who regularly came to dress his father's hair at home. With each new hair tweaked, Gallien stifled a pathetic moan. What an actor! If he weren't a merchant, he could have had a career on the stage!

The man at the door looked inside the shop, then came in and studied each of the clients. As he approached Maximus and Gallien, Maximus took a hot towel and vigorously rubbed the merchant's head. The man looked carefully at Maximus, who was careful to turn his head away and avoid his glance.

"Careful," the man said. "You'll twist his head off if you go on like that."

"Oh… of course, excuse me," Maximus stammered, keeping his eyes lowered. "I'm still just an apprentice."

The man shrugged his shoulders, eyed the shop for one last time, turned on his heels and left. When Maximus considered he must be far enough away, he stood up straight, breathed a sigh of relief, and signaled to Gallien to follow him.

"Hey!" the barber called after them as they were leaving. "Where's my money?"

"But we didn't get a haircut," Maximus pointed out.

"Quite right, and I can call back the man who just left and tell him that."

Maximus wrinkled his nose and looked at Gallien.

"Can you pay him?" he asked.

"Me? But I…"

"I haven't got any money on me."

Gallien protested but put his hands in his pockets and found a few sesterces.

"That's highway robbery!" he shouted at the barber as Maximus hurried him away.

"Do come again, gentlemen," the barber laughed as he pocketed the money and watched them go.

XXVII

DUPED

"So how about that goblet?" Gallien asked.

Now that they were safe inside the house of Maximus' parents, the merchant was determined to get what he had taken such risks to obtain.

"What goblet?" asked Maximus, looking innocent.

"The one you promised me."

"The goblet...?" Maximus repeated, trying to buy time.

"You promised me!" Gallien insisted.

Maximus could see that the man who had saved their lives was far from the muscular, athletic figure he had imagined, Titus smiled and regained courage. He had nothing to fear from Gallien.

"We don't have it," he simply replied.

Gallien became agitated and shouted, "Liars! Give me that goblet!"

"Not possible," Titus said. "Septimus took it."

"But you told me..."

Gallien realized he had been duped. He stood up and rushed at Titus. He grabbed him by the throat and shook him.

"The goblet!" he shouted, "I want that goblet!"

Terrified, Titus gasped, "Help!"

Aghiles stepped in to ward off the hysterical merchant. "Septimus took the goblet from us," he repeated, holding Gallien back with a firm grip.

The merchant was purple with anger. "Are you telling me I went through all that for nothing! I risked my life for nothing! I knocked Septimus out for nothing?" Little by little his voice rose to a scream.

Maximus made a calming gesture and said in a soothing voice, "No, not for nothing. Just think, you saved our lives. My father will be deeply indebted to you."

"Mine too," Titus added in a raspy voice.

Gallien couldn't care less about anybody's gratitude. He was interested in one thing only.

"But that goblet—did you ever really have it in the first place?"

"Yes, we actually did have it," Maximus said. "But Septimus stole it from us. That's no doubt why he kidnapped us. But, in any case, I don't know if it's the one you're looking for."

Gallien gave him a suspicious look. "But I heard you in the library talking about a goblet."

Maximus shot a look at Aghiles. Now they understood how Gallien had found out about the object. What a stroke of luck that he had overheard them and followed them. Otherwise, they would still be stuck in the bowels of that damp cellar.

"Yes, of course we were speaking about a goblet," Maximus continued. "But how do we know it's the one you're looking for?"

"Very simple: it's made of agate. There's no other like it."

"On the contrary, it seems to me its great simplicity is just what makes it difficult to identify."

"Oh, that!" Gallien replied with a wave of his hand. "I don't need anything to be able to identify it. I just know."

"What do you know?"

Maximus was careful not to show just how interested he was, to avoid arousing Gallien's suspicions. This was his chance to discover at last what this goblet was and why it was so coveted. But Gallien looked at him with a defiant air. He hadn't yet obtained the object of his desire. Until then, he wasn't saying anything.

XXVIII

AMNESIA

When Septimus opened his eyes, everything was a blur. He couldn't make out the shape of the room, and the floor seemed to float and shift around him. He felt nauseous. His mouth was pasty. He couldn't quite figure out where he was. Above all, he couldn't remember what had happened to him. He raised himself with difficulty onto his elbow, and then to his knees. He shook his head. Everything was spinning around him. He took a deep breath and then stood all the way up. He didn't know this room; he didn't recognize the furniture.

There were things scattered on the floor. A statuette, in particular. There had been a struggle here. The shooting pains in his head were proof of that. The street door was wide open. Septimus went to close it. He cast an eye up and down the little street, but he didn't recognize that either. This feeling of not being where he ought to be was distinctly disagreeable.

Just as he was about to shut the door, a man rushed toward him.

"Septimus!" the man shouted as he entered, but then stopped dead in his tracks. On finding Septimus, he instinctively froze. "Are you all right, Septimus? I... I... I'm so sorry. I saw you on the ground, but I had to follow them. You understand, don't you?"

Septimus gave him an odd look. He had no idea what this man was talking about.

"Who are you?" he asked.

The man couldn't hide his amazement. "Septimus," he repeated, "are you all right?"

"I'm not sure I really remember anything," Septimus admitted with a grimace of pain.

The man stared at him for a long moment before his face relaxed.

"You don't know who I am?" he asked.

Septimus shook his head.

The man smiled. That suited him just fine.

"I don't know who I am either or what I'm doing here. I must have been in a fight. Or someone attacked me."

"Unbelievable," the man murmured. He took Septimus by the arm and, with a honeyed smile on his face, encouraged him to follow him. "Come get some rest. Come, this way."

Septimus let himself be guided without resistance. That wasn't like him, but, to tell the truth, he wasn't quite himself. He couldn't understand what was going on, and the man speaking to him seemed unwilling to explain what had happened.

"Don't worry," the man reassured him. "Everything will look better in the morning."

He settled Septimus in one of the bedrooms in the house. Without losing a moment, he rushed to what really was Septimus' bedroom. If before the ex-gladiator regained his memory, he could find the goblet and deliver it to the emperor, he could take credit for the discovery and reap the reward. It would then be the good life for him, and freedom, far away from Septimus and his tyranny.

XXIX

THE STAKEOUT

The soldier carefully studied the surroundings. His chief had ordered him to keep the house under surveillance. He was to keep an eye on its inhabitants, the entrances and exits, any deliveries, and any movements in the area. He was used to this kind of duty. He was normally sent to spy on and unmask Christians or opponents of the emperor. But this time, it was a question of murder.

That said, in Rome there was nothing exceptional or surprising about a murder in the street. At that time, the crime rate in the capital of the Roman Empire was high, especially at night. The settling of scores was an everyday occurrence. Thefts gone wrong were commonplace. Nothing surprised the inhabitants anymore, especially the *urbaniciani*, who rarely ever solved a case.

Yet this case was different. To begin with, the city police had no idea of the victim's identity. They hadn't even seen the body. All they had to go on was what people were willing to tell them or the gossip they had heard doing their rounds.

Normally, a homicide like this, with nothing to go on, would have been immediately filed away. Except, in this case, the location where the victim had been found was awkward—right in front of the house of the renowned wild animal trader Flavius

Octavius, in one of the reputedly safest neighborhoods in the city.

Also, the victim had been seen outside his house earlier in the day. He had even been seen talking to the owner's son and his friends. And he had been followed when he left them.

The biggest mystery of all was that phony police officers had showed up to investigate and gather witness statements from the boys. These bogus *urbaniciani* had also removed the body, no doubt to avoid its identification. Then a stranger interested in the murder had showed up to ask questions, and a slave of Flavius Octavius had followed him to this house.

All of these disturbing facts led the police chief to order surveillance of the house. The man on duty was told to keep a lookout for that inquisitive stranger, who had set alarm bells ringing for Faustus, Flavius Octavius' right-hand man.

The soldier scouted out the ideal lookout position—a recess under a porch where he could keep an eye on the building without being seen. Of course, there was a bit of the façade he couldn't see, but that had only a narrow window no one could use as an entrance or an exit. He leaned against the door and bent his leg, adopting a comfortable position in which to keep watch. He knew he would be there for several hours before he could report back to the station. He had an excellent memory and no need to note things down. He never forgot a face.

Thanks to his mental cross-referencing of faces, he had managed to arrest many Christians. Some of them he wouldn't denounce but, rather, keep an eye on. Without realizing it, they would lead him to the hideouts of new believers. It was dirty work, and he knew it. But he didn't lose any sleep over it. It was just a job, a way of making a living. He kept a cool head and didn't dwell on the consequences of his denunciations. He remained totally detached, perfectly professional.

The soldier had only been at his post for a few minutes when someone came to the front door. A tall, strong man, square-shouldered and square-jawed, with a slightly droopy eyelid. He knocked at the door. It took some time for anyone to answer and speak to him through a crack in the door before letting him in. The man looked furtively around him and hurried into the house.

"Now there's someone who looks guilty," thought the soldier with a certain satisfaction. This was a good start. His instincts told him his presence there hadn't been a waste of time. And there was nothing he hated more than wasting time.

XXX

THE SEARCH

The man stopped in the doorway of the bedroom and watched Septimus sleeping. He hesitated.

He had gone through Septimus' room with a fine-tooth comb. He had turned everything upside down and moved the furniture around. But he found nothing. The goblet wasn't there. He had searched through the other rooms too. But there wasn't the slightest trace of the goblet there either. There was only one place he hadn't yet searched: Septimus himself!

The former gladiator was fast asleep. His breathing was regular. Asleep like that, he almost looked like a nice guy; with his curly blond hair, thick lips, and button-nose, he actually looked quite sweet.

The man tiptoed forward. He held his breath, trying to keep his heart from thumping so loudly. What if Septimus could hear it? Up close to Septimus, he eyed him carefully, looking for a bulge in his tunic, a bump, or anything sticking out a little. But it was hard to tell if what he saw was just a kneecap, a bunch of fabric, or a goblet hidden under his clothing.

He stretched his trembling hands toward Septimus. He swept his fingers lightly over his clothing. He clenched his teeth, not daring to handle him more vigorously. Then, he gently laid his hand on Septimus' shoulder.

If the gladiator opened his eyes now, his henchman could always explain he was just trying to wake him up. But Septimus didn't move. His heart seemed to skip a beat, then returned to an even rhythm. The man relaxed just a tiny bit and put his other hand on Septimus. Still no reaction. So he went a little further, gently patting his clothing down the length of his thigh, then back up across his chest. He leaned foward to reach his other shoulder when...

"Ahhhh...!" The man screamed in terror. Septimus had just clasped his arm in an iron grip.

"Looking for something?" Septimus growled, his voice full of menace.

The man gulped and tried to jump away. But Septimus had now dug his fingers into his skin.

"N-n-n-o," the man stammered. "I was just trying to wake you up."

"To wake me up... Don't give me that."

Still bent over Septimus, the man felt the ex-gladiator's hand come down violently on his ear. The dull thud pierced his eardrum, and a trickle of blood flowed out. The pain was intense. The man was terrified; the old Septimus was back again, crueler and more frightening than ever.

"Looking for something?" the ex-gladiator thundered again.

"The... the... the g-g-goblet," he stuttered. There was no point in lying. He was already done for anyway.

Septimus sat up, still grasping his arm and twisting it behind his back. With his free hand, he punched him on the chin. The man's jaw cracked. The taste of blood filled his mouth. He must have broken several teeth.

"The goblet?" Septimus repeated. Having rested, he was slowly starting to regain his memory. "You want it, do you?" he asked, twisting the man's arm further up.

The man groaned in pain. "No, no! I was just making sure they hadn't taken it."

"Who are 'they'?"

"Those... those boys."

A hint of doubt crossed Septimus' eyes. For a split second, he slightly eased his grip. The man moved sharply away, jumped back, and fled without a look behind him.

Septimus didn't even bother trying to follow him. The man had been so frightened that if he did have the goblet, he would have immediately surrendered it. Septimus absolutely must remember who "those boys" were and find that goblet.

XXXI

A SPUR-OF-THE-MOMENT DECISION

"You were right," said Titus. "If you hadn't promised him the goblet, Gallien would never have helped us."

The merchant had just left, but not before receiving the promise of a meeting with the fathers of Titus and Maximus. The boys suspected he wanted to negotiate a reward for his act of bravery.

"In any case, I'll just be glad when this whole thing is over," Titus said with a sigh. "A dead body and a kidnapping is more than enough for one day." He frowned, "I'm beginning to think perhaps you're right, Maximus."

"Right about...?"

"About the fortune-teller. He's not as good as he makes out." Maximus stifled a big smile.

"He predicted my day would turn out all right. Well, he got that wrong..."

Titus suddenly stopped and slapped his head. "But no!" he exclaimed. "I'm the one who got it wrong. He told me I should offer dates to the household gods! I forgot to do it, or at least I didn't have the time to. That wasn't the fortune-teller's fault!"

Titus could smile again. But Maximus just shook his head and sighed.

"When will you ever stop making excuses for him?" Maximus rebuked his friend. "That man is nothing more than a charlatan. He takes advantage of gullible people like you to get rich."

"Rich! Have you seen his clothing? On the contrary, he's poor!"

"That's what he wants you to think. No doubt, to make you feel sorry for him."

"You're talking nonsense."

"Unless he's so stingy, he doesn't even deign to buy clean clothes and go to the public baths."

Titus gave a disdainful shrug of the shoulders.

If there was a subject these two friends would never agree on, this was it. Titus was well versed in all the beliefs of the time. He prayed to the *lares*, the household gods, whose anger he feared. He never left the house without his *bulla*, his protective amulet. He was careful never to enter a house on his left foot and never to blaspheme. He honored the emperor as though he were divine.

For his part, Maximus was neither pious nor superstitious like his friend. He limited himself to the practices required of a good Roman citizen, in the eyes of others. There was no conviction in his prayers, and he gave no credence to the offerings he was occasionally forced to make. Titus adhered to the Roman religion more through fear and duty than real conviction. Maximus ignored it through lack of interest.

"In any case, you don't respect anything that has to do with religion," Titus sighed.

Maximus looked away to cut the conversation short. He didn't want to rehash that old argument again.

"Fine...," Titus concluded. He didn't want to argue either. "How about if we go get something to eat in the Forum to celebrate?"

"Celebrate what?"

"The end of this whole sorry story."

Maximus pursed his lips in a mischievous little smile.

"It's just that... it isn't really...," he replied, slipping his hand under his tunic.

And with that, he pulled out the famous goblet everyone was after. Titus' and Aghiles' eyes popped out in surprise.

"But... but... you're completely crazy!" Titus stammered.

"Calm down," Maximus reassured him. "No one knows I'm the one who has it."

"And may we know how—"

"Septimus had it on him," Maximus said, stopping his friend before he finished his sentence. "I saw it sticking out of his tunic when I leaned over him to check if he was still breathing. I couldn't resist taking the goblet back."

"So why didn't you give it to Gallien?" Aghiles asked. "He deserves it. He helped us escape."

"I know," he agreed, looking sheepish. "I considered it, but in the end I didn't. I don't know why, but I just didn't have the heart to give it to him. It was as though something was holding me back. And I need to know why."

"Don't you realize the danger you've placed us in?" Titus angrily shouted.

"I promise you, I'll hide it carefully till then."

"Till when?"

"Till I give it back to its rightful owner."

"But he's dead!" Titus' voice had now almost risen to a screech.

"I'm not so sure..."

"What nonsense you're talking!"

"But how do we know that dead man was the owner of this goblet? And exactly what do we know about this goblet?"

"Don't play the smart guy with us," said Titus with mounting anger. "That goblet goes to Gallien, and that's that. What's more, he knows where it comes from. He knows what it's worth."

"But he didn't want to tell us anything."

"So what?"

"I agree with Titus," Aghiles interrupted in a somber voice. "That goblet should go to Gallien."

Maximus frowned. His two friends disagreed with him, and that pained him. He realized he should indeed have given the merchant the goblet as agreed. And yet, he just couldn't. He would think about it again tomorrow.

"In the meantime, I've got to hide the goblet," he said. "I'll come see you tomorrow, Titus. We'll talk about it again then."

"There's nothing more to talk about!" snapped Titus. "Tomorrow it will be in the hands of Gallien, and we'll say no more about it!"

XXXII

THE HIDEOUT DISCOVERED

The soldier stretched his neck and worked his shoulders up and down to ease his aching back. He had been watching the house for a while now, and his muscles were starting to stiffen. A little exercise wouldn't hurt, but he couldn't leave his post.

He had, though, gleaned quite a bit of intelligence over the past hours. He was now sure that this house was a Christian hideout. While he had watched the door, he had seen many comings and goings—many more than for a normal house. Even the most prominent people in the city didn't receive as many people—not to mention so many visitors looking anxious and rushed. They would look to the right and the left before entering. Whenever a soldier entered the street, they would turn around and pretend to be busy elsewhere. Whoever was inside that house showed the same wariness. The door was never opened wide. Whoever was inside was careful to remain in the shadows.

This officer of the *urbaniciani* now had enough information to make a detailed report to his superior. He was sure they would send a troop to arrest a bunch of these people. The emperor would be pleased. He would have lots of Christians to throw to the lions at the next circus games.

Nevertheless, the soldier wouldn't be going home quite yet. His mission hadn't been to unearth Christians, and it wasn't up to him to question orders. He had been sent to assist in the investigation of the murder in front of the house of Flavius Octavius. And, on that matter, he had made no progress. On that score, he hadn't the slightest lead.

He had been briefed about a dark-complexioned man, an African, who was thought to have visited the house of Flavius Octavius and might be involved, but the soldier hadn't seen him. It was almost as though he had been given the wrong address. He gave a sigh. He was all right to stay there for another few hours. Luckily, it looked as though the nighttime weather was going to be mild. At least he wouldn't be cold.

Just a few yards away from him, right inside that very same house, the African was nervous. Tiburtius had come earlier to inform him that there had been no news on the goblet and that, for his part, he hadn't been able to find Titus, Maximus, or Aghiles.

Hopes of getting the goblet back were dwindling. The leads were getting thin. What's worse, the African realized he had been very imprudent going to the house of Flavius Octavius. Ready to do anything to find the goblet, he had left the house without taking enough precautions. Now he feared he may have cast suspicion on Faustus.

XXXIII

FRUSTRATION

Septimus woke up fit and full of energy. He was back to his old self—that is to say, violent, determined, cruel, and without a conscience. He had only one little problem: the terrible blow to his head had erased his memory of what had happened to him and why.

Septimus wandered through all the many rooms of the house in the hope of finding some detail that would unlock his brain and bring his memory flooding back.

The ex-gladiator tried to recall the key elements, without which he couldn't carry out his mission. He knew he was supposed to bring a goblet to Emperor Diocletian. And he remembered that he had been following a certain Delitilis, but everything else was a blank.

The body of Delitilis, his own false police identity, the testimony of Titus and his friends, their kidnapping, and their escape—none of that he remembered. At moments, bits of it came back to him, but nothing to help him see the full picture. And, worse than that, he had no idea where that goblet was. The man he caught searching him—whose name he couldn't recall either—also seemed to be looking for it. He mentioned that "those boys" might have taken it. But what boys?

"Arrgh!"

Septimus banged his head against the wall. If only he could get his blasted memory back, because there was one thing he hadn't forgotten: he must succeed. If he failed in this mission, the emperor would never forgive him.

XXXIV

FORGIVENESS

When he arrived at Titus' house the next day, Maximus had dark rings under his eyes. He had hardly slept all night. He couldn't stop going over the events of the previous day, trying to understand what it was that had made him take the goblet and hold on to it. He couldn't find any explanation—in any case, no rational explanation, just a vague feeling of urgency.

"You look terrible," Titus said icily. "Has your conscience been keeping you up all night?"

Maximus didn't take the bait. He understood his friend's annoyance. After all, it had already been his fault that Septimus had kidnapped them. If Maximus had just given up the goblet in the first place, when they had been questioned by that phony police officer, none of this would have happened. And now that Titus knew Maximus still had the goblet, he once again felt in danger. And, what's worse, his peril was because of his best friend—that's what really hurt.

"Forgive me, Titus," Maximus mumbled. "I couldn't help myself. I shouldn't have done it."

"You can say that again! Do you realize Septimus knows my address?"

Titus bit his tongue. As he was speaking, he suddenly remembered that he had told the old gladiator where Maximus lived.

133

He was under threat, that's true, but he had still revealed it.

"You're right," Maximus continued, not noticing Titus' hesitation. "We'll give the goblet to Gallien. And we'll let it be known so that we don't get into any more trouble. Then he can do what he wants with it."

Smiling with relief, Titus said, "You've come to your senses at last."

Maximus shrugged his shoulders. "Let's just say I couldn't live with myself if anything else happened to you because of me."

Titus reached out his hand and warmly clasped his friend's shoulder. That's what he liked about his friendship with Maximus: their arguments never lasted very long. Standing a little to one side, Aghiles too gave a little smile. Now everything could get back to normal, and that's the way he liked things.

"You'll never guess who came to see us," said Titus to change the subject.

"Who?"

"Gratus."

Maximus wrinkled his brow, trying to remember who Gratus was. "No! Gratus? Our sea captain?"[1]

Titus nodded. "At least I suppose that's who the visitor was. Faustus told me a certain Gratus stopped by yesterday. Who else could it be but the man who ferried us across *mare nostrum*?"[2]

"And what did he want?" asked Maximus, surprised by this visit. "I never thought we would see that outlandish sea captain again."

---

1. See volume 2, *A Lion for the Emperor.*
2. Literally, "our sea," what the Romans called the Mediterranean.

Titus nodded with amusement and explained, "He came to offer me his condolences."

"What?!"

"I had the same reaction. And Faustus as well. Gratus thought the body found in front of our house must have been a relative. What a strange man he is..."

As Titus went on chuckling about this funny situation, Maximus couldn't help thinking that Gratus' visit perhaps wasn't so surprising as that. After all, he wouldn't be the first to show an interest in this mysterious goblet.

"Did he say he would come back?" Maximus asked, lost in thought.

"I don't think so. But to know for sure, you need to ask Faustus."

A few minutes later, Maximus found an excuse to leave Titus and Aghiles on their own and go find Faustus. From the moment he had heard Gratus' name, he couldn't get him out of his head. He needed to find out the real reason behind his visit.

Maximus found Faustus just where he thought he would be: in the office of Flavius Octavius, taking care of daily business in his employer's absence.

"Good morning, Faustus," he greeted him.

The old man looked up and smiled. He was fond of Maximus. He had to admire the boy's dynamism despite his slight build.

"Maximus! I'm delighted to see you."

"To tell you the truth, Faustus, I'm here to ask you something."

The old man gave an even broader smile. He also liked this boy's frankness.

"I'm listening."

"Titus tells me that Gratus came here yesterday."

"That's right," Faustus confirmed. "Titus was disappointed to have missed him."

"I too!" Maximus exclaimed.

"Well, as for me, I was a bit suspicious of him. So many strange things happened yesterday. Did you know, for example, that those *urbaniciani* who were here...?"

"You mean Septimus Demetrius and his men?"

"Yes. Well, in fact they were fake *urbaniciani*. The real ones arrived much later. They'd been held up on another case."

"No!" Maximus feigned astonishment. "Do you know why they were here?"

"I don't know," replied Faustus, shaking his head. "In any case, it put me on my guard. And when Gratus arrived, I immediately thought he looked suspicious. At first, I almost took him for a slave."

"Gratus, a slave? He's far too fat for that!" exclaimed Maximus with amusement.

"Really? He didn't look overweight to me... No, it was his dark complexion that fooled me," Faustus admitted. "In Rome, it's rare to meet an African who isn't a slave."

Maximus gave a start. Gratus? An African? Something didn't add up here.

"Anyway," Faustus went on, not noticing Maximus' troubled look, "I was relieved to hear you really did know him. That's one less person for me to be wary of in the future."

"I really would have liked to see him again. We hardly had time to say a proper goodbye when we arrived at the port. Did he leave you his address?"

"No, he left without even leaving a message for you."

Maximus frowned. This was all very strange. Gratus didn't look anything like an African, and he was far too simple a person to be so mysterious. Also, he would have left an address where they could find him.

Faustus gave him a mischievous smile. "He didn't leave any message," he continued, "but as I didn't trust him, I had him followed."

Maximus' face brightened.

"So you know where he lives?"

Faustus winked and gave Maximus the address.

With the knowledge of Gratus' location, Maximus returned to his friends. "I have to go out; I need to find a present for my mother," he told them. "I'll be right back."

Aghiles was up like a shot to follow his friend and master.

"Go back home, Aghiles," Maximus said. "I don't need you, and I won't be long."

And before his slave had time to reply, he was off.

XXXV

NEGOTIATIONS

Gallien couldn't decide how to present himself at Titus' home. The boy had said he would send for him as soon as his father returned, but the merchant preferred to take the initiative himself. Above all, he didn't want those boys to forget about him. Of the three, Gallien had quickly understood, Titus would be the easiest for him to manipulate, and the most approachable as well. With the monkey constantly perched on his shoulder, Titus had a very friendly look that inspired confidence. Maximus seemed to him a cooler customer, less good-humored and, above all, much more sure of himself. As for Aghiles, he was only a slave, so he didn't count, as far as he was concerned.

Gallien got out his best toga. He wanted to make a good impression. After all, Flavius Octavius was a very prominent person in Rome. Once dressed, Gallien checked his appearance in a tall *speculum*.[1] He passed his fingers through his hair and patted it in place. He smiled at his reflection. His last-minute visit to the hairdresser the day before had paid off. You couldn't see one white hair anymore. Gallien sucked in his stomach and held his breath. Then he breathed out, looked at himself again, and shook his head with a frown.

"It's no good!"

---

1. A mirror made of polished metal.

His toga was too luxurious. Titus' father might take him for a wealthy merchant—which, after all, he was—and lower his reward. Gallien suddenly wondered if it might be better to play on his sympathy to get more money out of him.

When Gallien arrived at the door of Titus' house a little later, he was a different man. He had rejected his finest toga in favor of a very simple, slightly frayed tunic. His hair was no longer perfectly in place, but tousled. If he wanted to arouse pity, this was the look to assure success. Even a bit too successful—for the shoes on his feet were so full of holes, they made the merchant walk with a limp. There was now a pebble stuck in the sole that he couldn't get out and hurt him with every step.

"Gallien?!"

Titus was astonished to see him on his doorstep.

"I've come to call on Flavius Octavius," replied Gallien in a honeyed tone.

"But he's not here. I told you. I said I'd send for you."

"I just stopped by on the off chance...," Gallien said apologetically.

Titus hesitated a moment, then smiled. He wasn't a total dupe and suspected Gallien was trying to make sure he hadn't forgotten him. Whatever the case, he had arrived at the right moment.

"To tell the truth, it's good you've come," he said. "We've found the goblet."

Gallien's eyes widened in surprise. He licked his lips with a greedy smile.

"The goblet?"

"Yes, we managed to get it back."

Gallien couldn't believe his ears.

"But how? Septimus..."

There was no question of betraying Maximus' deceit. So Titus decided to make up a story.

"Well, it wasn't easy," he admitted with a dramatic sigh. "Obviously, he resisted."

"How do you mean?"

"Yesterday, after you left, we decided to take our property back. Sorry, I mean *your* property."

Gallien straightened up, flattered by such respect.

"Between you and me, Aghiles can be very persuasive when he gets angry," Titus continued in a conspiratorial tone. "And he did get angry. He gave Septimus what was coming to him..."

Gallien couldn't hide his amazement. He could hardly believe Septimus would give up so easily against a kid of fifteen, maybe seventeen.

"It must be said," Titus went on to calm Gallien's doubts, "the bang on the head you gave him really weakened him."

The merchant puffed up with pride. So this victory was a little thanks to him.

"How wonderful!" he exclaimed. "Can I see the goblet?"

"Well, er...," said Titus, a little uncomfortably. "We ran a lot of risks..."

"But you said I'd put Septimus out of action...," Gallien began, worried that Titus was backpedaling.

"Septimus, yes. But not the others."

"The others?"

"Oh, at least a dozen of them," said Titus, enjoying his own story.

"No!"

"And nasty ones at that."

"And then what?" Gallien asked.

"It was one hell of a fight, I can tell you. I'm still aching all over. So... we'd like to go fifty-fifty with you on the goblet."

Gallien made a face. So that was it. He knew it had been too good to be true.

"It's just that... I'm not sure I'll be able to sell it," he replied with feigned meekness. He was glad now of his choice of clothing. "You can see life's not very easy for me..."

"You seemed pretty sure of yourself yesterday."

"Oh, you know how it is. It's easy to talk until you get down to brass tacks." Gallien was thinking fast. "What about a little cash in exchange," he proposed.

"Hmmm..."

"A thousand sesterces."

Titus looked offended. "That's nothing! You'll get ten times that much for it.

"Two thousand then?"

Titus wrinkled his nose.

"Three thousand?" Gallien suggested.

Titus held back a smile. Three thousand sounded reasonable to him.

"I need to think about it," he said.

"Three thousand five hundred sesterces!" Gallien said with finality. "I can deliver it to you tomorrow afternoon. I need time to get the money together."

Titus made him wait for an answer, playing on Gallien's nerves. Then finally, he announced, "It's a deal. Bring me the money, and then I'll give you the goblet."

Gallien was about to leave when Titus grabbed him by the sleeve of his frayed tunic. "We'll keep this between ourselves, right?"

"That goes without saying," Gallien said as he left.

Three thousand five hundred sesterces, thought Titus. That's not too high a price to pay for all we've been through.

XXXVI

GRATUS

"Yes?" said someone on the other side of the door.

"I've come to see Gratus," Maximus called.

"I'm sorry, there's no Gratus here." The voice was friendly but firm.

"I was told he was here. He called yesterday wanting to see me."

"I don't know who you're talking about. There's no one called Gratus here."

Maximus hesitated. He took a step back, looked at the house, and returned to the door. He wasn't mistaken: this was the address Faustus had given him.

"My name is Maximus," he whispered again through the door. "Can you let him know I'm here?"

"I repeat, I know no one called Gratus. Would you kindly go away please."

The voice had now become nervous. Maximus could hear someone moving behind the door. He had to try a different approach.

"I arrived with him here from Leptis Magna. On the boat... With the lion..."

A deep silence followed these words. The person was thinking. "Wait!" he at last shouted.

Maximus again took a step back. He looked around him, at the street, the passersby. There was a man standing under a neighboring porch, some women walking by, shops a little further along the street. The creaking door made him turn around.

"Come in," someone hurriedly whispered.

Maximus slipped through the half-open door into the house. He immediately found himself in a light-filled atrium. In the middle, a fountain filled the air with the crystalline music of flowing water.

"Follow me," said the man who had let him in.

He was tall, with an athletic build, angular features, and an eye that peered at Maximus strangely. A little scar made one eyelid droop lower than the other. The man walked ahead of Maximus, but the boy could sense he was on the alert. At the least suspicious move, Maximus thought, the man would pin him to the ground. They crossed the sunny atrium and entered a room at the back of the house, an office, or perhaps a bedroom. The furnishings were so sparse it was hard to tell. A man was seated on the floor with his back to them.

"Antimus," called the man escorting Maximus.

The man seated on the floor slowly turned around. Maximus gave a start as he recognized him. And on seeing Maximus, the African's face lit up as well. He quickly rose and went to the boy with open arms.

"Maximus, my friend!"

Maximus carefully studied him. Not too tall, with a dark complexion, and brown eyes. He was just as he remembered him.

"Gratus?!" Maximus mischievously teased. "Antimus? And I thought your name was Justinian!"

Antimus smiled.

"My real name is Antimus. I went by the name of Justinian during our sea journey. I was afraid someone might sound the alarm when they heard I was headed for Rome. But, please, take a seat. I'm glad you've come."

"And how does Gratus figure in all this?"

"It was the first name that came into my head when I went to Titus' house."

Antimus smiled and sat down again. Maximus took the seat facing him. Behind him, he could feel the presence of the man who had let him in. He remained standing on guard, ready to step in should anything go wrong.

Antimus gave a good long look at the boy before him. He found him decisive and self-assured, his eyes sparkling with intelligence.

"I heard that you'd visited the house of Flavius Octavius," Maximus began, wishing to get straight to the point. "You'd apparently come to offer your condolences to Titus!"

Antimus smiled again. "That's true. I thought someone close to him had been murdered. Fortunately, that wasn't the case."

Now it was Maximus' turn to weigh up the man before him. While on the boat, Maximus had admired his courage and good sense. He had always been ready to help everyone, and he had saved Titus' father from disgrace even though his arrest would have been to Antimus' advantage. Today, Maximus found the man he had known aboard the ship composed and friendly.

"I won't beat around the bush, Antimus," he said finally. "I don't think you came just to offer your condolences to Titus. You know as well as I do that Titus had nothing to do with that murdered man."

"Nothing to do with him?" Antimus repeated with a hint of disappointment in his voice.

Maximus shook his head. "No, nothing."

Antimus gave a long sigh. "Oh, I had hoped..."

Maximus let the silence settle before leaning forward and whispering, "Were you looking for something?"

Antimus stiffened slightly. He thought quickly, weighing up the situation. That one question was enough to pique his curiosity. Unless this boy knew about the goblet, why would he have asked that?

"Maximus," he began slowly, "I know I can trust you. Can't I?"

Maximus remained silent, still staring Antimus straight in the eye.

"When we were aboard Gratus' ship, you didn't denounce me, even though you knew who I was. You could have, but you didn't."

Maximus said nothing, but his whole body was straining forward.

"Yes, I was looking for something," Antimus admitted.

"An agate goblet perhaps?" Maximus then asked with a half smile.

The man behind him suddenly stiffened. As for Antimus, he tried to restrain a smile, but he struggled to hide his surprise. He placed his hands on his knees and took a deep breath. There was no point in pretending anymore.

"How do you know? Have you seen it?" he asked as calmly as he could.

Maximus nodded. "I've even held it in my hands. A couple of days ago, a man asked us for directions. We didn't know who he was. He approached us and took advantage of the moment to slip the agate goblet into Titus' sack. The next day, we found him dead on Titus' doorstep."

"Delitilis," the man behind Maximus whispered under his breath.

Maximus turned to him, at a loss.

"The man...," murmured this guard dog, "the man who was murdered.... His name was Delitilis."

Maximus turned back to Antimus, who explained the role of this thief from Hispania. He didn't omit any detail, in order to help Maximus understand. But he struggled to contain the one question burning on his lips.

"And do you still have it?" he whispered at last.

"No," Maximus replied. "Someone posing as a policeman took it from us. His name is Septimus, an ex-gladiator."

"The most fearsome of them all," the guard behind him said with a groan.

Antimus shot him a quizzical look.

"If Septimus has it," the guard continued, "we've no chance of getting it back. He'll take it to the emperor. Septimus has become Diocletian's henchman."

Antimus held his head in his hands and slowly rubbed his temple.

"I'm very sorry," Maximus whispered after a moment.

Antimus took a deep gulp. "There's nothing to be done. It's just that, when I saw you, I had hoped..."

"Is this goblet really that important to you?"

Antimus looked at Maximus in stupefaction.

"So you don't know, then?"

XXXVII

THE MYSTERY REVEALED

Antimus remained silent for a moment. Maximus waited, in suspense, hanging on his words.

"You must think it's just a goblet like any other," Antimus finally said. "No more special than any other. And, no doubt, based on its appearance, you'd be right. I don't know. I've never seen it. And yet, in the eyes of us Christians, it's priceless. The deacon Lawrence sent it to Hispania in the year 258 for safe-keeping. It has now been returned to Rome. And the emperor wants it destroyed. Not happy just to persecute us, he wants to destroy every symbol of the Christian faith. That goblet... —Antimus paused a moment, mastering his emotion—that goblet is the Holy Chalice."

"The Holy Chalice?" The words didn't mean anything to Maximus.

Seeing his friend's confusion, Antimus explained, "It's the cup in which Jesus turned wine into his blood at the Last Supper."

Maximus held back a scowl of disgust.

"So it's true," he said, that story about Jesus giving his friends his body and blood to eat and drink?"

Not understanding the mystery of the Eucharist, a good many Romans considered Christians cannibals because of this. For his part, Maximus never listened to people's gossip. But now that Antimus himself, a Christian, was telling him this, he no longer knew what to think.

Antimus smiled. "Don't listen to what people say," he went on, as though he could read the boy's mind. "The bread and the wine that Jesus gave his Apostles to eat on the night of his Last Supper still had the appearance of bread and wine. But Jesus, who could do anything—because, as we Christians believe, he is God—transformed that bread and wine mysteriously into himself. He took their form in order to offer himself to those he loved—and not just at that moment, but for all time."

"And that's what this goblet would have been used for?" said Maximus with astonishment.

"There's nothing magical about it," Antimus continued with a gentle smile. "The Holy Chalice is one of the only relics that links us physically to our Lord Jesus Christ. Seeing it is a little like seeing him, feeling ourselves closer to him, the way you feel when you look at something given to you by a loved one who has now departed."

"Yet you tell me not much has been seen of this goblet, since it's been hidden away in Hispania," Maximus remarked.

"That's right. And if we manage to get it back, we will hide it again.

Just knowing it exists somewhere encourages our faith in Jesus. Perhaps one day we will be able to reveal this goblet to all, and then even more people will come to believe that the Son of God entered human history, as Jesus, to be our Savior."

As he spoke, Antimus' face lit up. His cheeks colored, and his eyes burned with fervor.

"Forgive me," he apologized. "I'm getting emotional."

He stood up. "I must leave you," he said. "I'm expected elsewhere. Even if you didn't bring the news I was hoping for, I'm happy you came. Thank you."

Maximus too stood up. Within seconds, he was back outside. The street looked the same. The man on the porch across the street still hadn't moved, but other women were strolling by here and there.

Inside the house, Tiburtius turned to Antimus, his brow wrinkled with anxiety.

"You were very incautious, Antimus!" he insisted. "I'm afraid we may have to move elsewhere."

"No, rest assured. I have total confidence in Maximus. I spent many days with him on the ship. He could have denounced me then, but he didn't."

"It's not him I'm worried about."

Antimus looked at Tiburtius; he didn't understand what he meant.

"You gave him your address!" Tiburtius reproached him.

"No, no. Absolutely not. You can't really think I'd do such a thing."

"So how do you explain how he found us?"

XXXVIII

ROAMING THE STREETS

Septimus was roaming the streets of Rome, trying to jog his memory. He felt strangely torn: On the one hand, he was itching for battle, to act. On the other hand, he felt a kind of weariness he couldn't manage to shake off. And perhaps a little fear as well? No, not Septimus. He had never been afraid, not even at the height of his career as a gladiator.

If he failed in his mission, the emperor would order his execution. That was a given. The emperor's trust could be lost as quickly as it could be won. Septimus accepted that. He wasn't afraid of death. He by far preferred that to dishonor. Anything was better than dishonor. In the arena, he had never felt anything but contempt for a rival who crawled and begged at his feet. He despised those who lowered themselves like that. In one sense, he almost admired the Christians whose persecution he sometimes attended. What dignity when faced with death! What courage!

As he walked in search of he knew not what, Septimus noticed a strangely familiar figure. A man, tall and athletic, was walking toward him without noticing him. Instinctively, Septimus hid to observe him as he walked by. Septimus recognized that drooping eyelid. Tiburtius!

They had met back in the days when they were both gladiators. Tiburtius had been as formidable as Septimus, and

Septimus would have liked to have squared off against him. But fate had decided otherwise. They never fought one another.

One day, when Tiburtius had an opponent at the point of his sword, he let him go. He reached out his hand and helped the man to his feet! The crowd booed him; one of the spectators threw a stone that just missed taking his eye out. But Tiburtius had simply turned his head. And he never entered the arena again. People said someone must have paid him never to fight again.

"What a waste!" Septimus thought to himself. "I would have liked to take him on!"

Just as Septimus was musing on this, another thought crossed his mind.

"But I did take him on, once. I remember now: Tiburtius had been following Delitilis too."

Everything now became clear. Septimus could see himself again shadowing Delitilis with Tiburtius at his heels. Septimus was jubilant. His memory was now coming back to him in waves. He could remember again that house, where Delitilis had stopped to ask for directions and where later the crowd gathered like flies to see his corpse. He recalled the money he had paid to bribe a few poor dupes to let him pass as one of the *urbaniciani*...

Septimus stopped at the street corner to think. His head was spinning. So many memories came flooding back to him, that he was afraid of forgetting any of them.

Little by little, he pieced together these recent events. And now, he could recall those three boys. No doubt the same boys he had been told about earlier. And the address of Titus, the boy with the monkey, also came back to him. He also remembered his friend Maximus, whose address he had extracted from

Titus under threat. Septimus gave a bloodthirsty laugh. He could carry out his mission after all.

With that, Septimus was off. He must catch up with Tiburtius, find out where he was going. He ran through the crowd and soon spotted the tall, massive figure of his old comrade-in-arms. Only then did he slow down to follow him at a distance. Tiburtius kept looking around him, behind him. As he was so tall, he sidled close to the walls, slouching down to better melt into the crowd.

After a moment, Tiburtius at last slowed his pace. He turned into a side street and began carefully observing every house. Suddenly, he came to a halt. He studied the housefront before him, raised his hand to knock at the door... but then stopped and reconsidered before crossing the street again, to observe the house. Trying to look as inconspicuous as possible, he feigned interest in a shop display.

Just a little further away, Septimus was mulling this over. The house that had caught Tiburtius' attention was the house of Maximus, whom he had kidnapped the day before but who had escaped. Was it possible that Maximus and Tiburtius knew one another? Would that explain why Delitilis had stopped those three boys? Septimus began to wonder. In the end, Titus was perhaps quite a little actor. Too many things all led to the same conclusion.

XXXIX

UNEASE

Aghiles paced back and forth like a caged animal as he waited for Maximus to return. He hated inaction. Everything that had happened involving that goblet left him with a vague feeling of uneasiness and worry. His hunter's instincts told him there was danger.

To begin with, he didn't trust Septimus. Having weighed him up, Aghiles was clear what kind of man he was. He was like an enraged lion that would stop at nothing. And then there was Gallien. Even though the escape of Aghiles and his friends was all thanks to him, Aghiles still didn't trust him. There was something fishy about that antique dealer. He seemed just a little too nice. He smiled with one side of his face while calculating with the other. He had only gotten involved for what he could gain. If the wind changed, he would be quick to change too.

But what really bothered Aghiles in this whole story was his best friend, Maximus. He couldn't understand his friend's attitude, his exposing them again to danger, his air of mystery, and his brushing aside his trustworthy slave and friend. Aghiles and Maximus shared a taste for risk and adventure, but this time, the situation was more dangerous than ever. There had already been one murder, and Aghiles was sure that those who had killed once wouldn't hesitate to kill again.

As he paced past the window, Aghiles cast a look outside and gave a start. Something immediately caught his attention, a scene he seemed to have seen before. He stopped and carefully observed the form of a man bent over the wares of a shop on the other side of the street, one of those countless shops found everywhere in the city of Rome. The way he held himself, his build, and that edginess he exuded too... Everything was the same as two days ago.

This was the same person who had been following the man found dead on Titus' doorstep. And now he was on the lookout in front of Maximus' house. This couldn't be a coincidence. Aghiles trembled. If this man were the murderer, his presence there now did not bode well.

XL

PACKING THEIR BAGS

Antimus reluctantly gathered up his things. Tiburtius wanted them to move, but Antimus wanted to stay put. His assistant's worries didn't seem well-founded to him. It was true, he couldn't explain how Maximus managed to find out where he lived, but he didn't consider the young man a potential threat. Maximus knew Antimus was a Christian, but he had nothing to gain by coming to find him.

And then, what had Tiburtius gained by standing guard outside Maximus' house? Nothing, absolutely nothing. Maximus had gone back home and hadn't left since. If he was up to something, he surely would have betrayed some nervousness.

Antimus sighed. This whole business of the Holy Grail was becoming more complicated. Everyone seemed to be after it. No one was behaving normally. Even he wasn't acting like himself. He was neglecting his own safety and putting himself at risk. Antimus, as a priest of the Christian community, attracted many of the faithful. They came to meet with him, to receive the sacraments. Antimus was a kind of magnet, and he was well aware that if he were arrested, many others would be taken along with him. That was why he had agreed to follow Tiburtius' advice to leave the premises—for the sake of all his brothers and sisters in the faith, not for himself.

They couldn't leave by night. That would be much too risky. Tiburtius thought the house was being watched. They had to find another hideout.

Outside, the man who had been staking them out for almost two days was no longer there.

The soldiers who had patrolled the street during their rounds had been ordered back to their barracks. Upon their return, the head of the patrol, the centurion Sertor, questioned the soldier on guard. "Anything to report?" he asked, getting right to the point.

The soldier lowered his eyes and replied, "Not as far as our investigation goes, no. The man we were watching hasn't left the house. Unless he found another way out."

It was just as the centurion suspected. Right from the start of this murder case, he had not one lead and was at a total loss. He hated that, but since he had been put in charge of the case, he couldn't leave any stone unturned. If the emperor were to find out he had neglected a request from Flavius Octavius, he could kiss his career goodbye.

"On the other hand," the soldier went on, "I think we'd do well to prepare a raid."

"On the house?"

"Yes, I'm sure it's a Christian safe house."

Centurion Sertor looked at him with interest. He knew this soldier well and could count on his instincts. So far, in their unit, he was the one who had arrested the most enemies of the emperor.

"And what do you suggest?"

"That we go in tonight. I think they may be getting ready to leave. I can tell they're jumpier than when I first arrived."

The centurion smiled with satisfaction.

"They're jumpy, you say? Well then, we'll make our move in the dead of night. Tell the men to get ready."

"I'll get right on it, Centurion Sertor," replied the soldier, clicking his heels.

The centurion stopped him. "How many men and women do you think are in the house?"

"I'd say there are four at night, but many more during the day."

"Take just ten men with you. That should be enough. The fewer of you there are, the less risk of alerting them."

XLI

AN INTRUDER

A little earlier that day, Septimus had done some scouting. Taking advantage of the crowds, he had made a tour of the whole block, looking for an easy, inconspicuous means of entering the house of Flavius Octavius. The branch of a fig tree hanging just over the street would allow him to climb onto a neighbor's roof. Since all the buildings were tightly packed together, he could easily crawl from there to Titus' house.

Septimus returned after nightfall. He had to be quick to climb up and hide before anyone saw him or, worse, before the night patrol passed by. He readied himself under the branch, bent his knees, and jumped up. With one great heave, he grasped hold of the branch and hoisted himself up. This was child's play for an athlete like him. He then inched along the branch to the wall. There was a rooftop terrace right in front of him. Without a sound, Septimus jumped onto the housetop and crouched down. No one could now see him from the street.

Septimus took time to observe his surroundings. Titus' house was the third one down from this one. The roofs almost all abutted one another, so it would be no trouble moving from one to the other. That left the question of what he would do when he arrived; he would have to go straight to his target. He could remember the layout of the rooms and where Titus' bedroom was. That was where he had questioned the boys while posing as one of the *urbaniciani*. The ex-gladiator smirked as he recalled that.

He would question Titus again, but this time with a bit more muscle. When he had first stopped the boy in the street, Titus had caved in at the first hint of menace. Titus had spilled everything to avoid having his finger broken. But now that he thought about it, Septimus wondered if Titus had been playing him. Ever since he had spotted Tiburtius, Septimus suspected Titus of playing a double game, of pretending to be more timid than he really was. After all, he and his friends had managed to escape from his clutches and, clearly, to steal the goblet back from him. That, Septimus could not forgive. No one had ever tricked him like that before. This time, Septimus wouldn't be so gullible. This time, the gloves were off. He knew a few nasty methods of torture that would make even the mute talk. Then it would be Maximus' turn.

Bent double, Septimus advanced across the rooftops. He inched slowly and silently forward. At the slightest sound of a voice or footsteps, he stopped, squatted down, and listened until he was sure the coast was clear. There was no one walking around on the housetops: the danger of being spotted came from below. Roman houses were all constructed around a central, open-air atrium from where he could be seen.

When he got to Titus' house, Septimus carefully peered down from the edge of the rooftop. He examined the atrium. It seemed to be empty. He noticed a corner in deep shadow. He would sneak in from there. As nimble as a snake despite his strong build, Septimus slithered down the wall holding on by his fingertips. When his feet could almost touch the ground, he let go and landed in the atrium with a muffled thud. He remained a moment crouched down, listening to the silence of the house. All was quiet. Septimus could hear a few snores coming from the rooms at the back of the house, perhaps the slaves' quarters. Or maybe from the room of the old man who had received him, thinking he was from the police.

Septimus glued himself to the wall, then carefully moved forward crouched down. There was only pale moonlight, and he struggled to make out the way before him. If he banged into anything or knocked something over, he risked waking the household. There was such total silence, the slightest noise could give him away.

Septimus walked by the first room, whose door was slightly ajar. He passed the second room, then the third, and finally stopped. This was Titus' bedroom. He remembered it clearly.

The door was closed, and without making a sound, Septimus grabbed the door handle. This was the critical moment. Once inside Titus' bedroom, Septimus knew he could overpower the boy in a split second, before he had time to fight back or scream. But opening the door was another matter. It might creak or scrape against the floor. And any little noise could give him away. Septimus placed both hands firmly on the handle, and, holding his breath, turned it. Click! The latch gave way. Inch by inch, Septimus pushed the door. When it was open wide enough, he slipped inside the bedroom and carefully closed the door behind him. He stopped a few seconds to catch his breath, then turned to the bed in the opposite corner.

XLII

THE SAME BRIGHT IDEA

Gallien pulled the cart against the wall and stopped. He looked up at the tree branch and frowned. It hadn't looked that high when he had made his reconnaissance earlier that day. But no matter—he wasn't going to let the first obstacle get in his way. He had been turning his plan over in his mind most of the day, convinced that he was within his rights to take the goblet without paying for it. After all, Titus, Maximus, and Aghiles had promised it to him. It was Titus who had gone back on his word and tried to extort money from him. Well, Gallien wasn't going to fall for that.

He climbed onto the cart, stood on tiptoe, and grabbed the branch of the fig tree.

"Oof!" he groaned, trying to hoist himself up onto the branch.

Footsteps below brought him tumbling back down to the ground. Gallien quickly got up and pretended he was pulling the cart along. There was nothing unusual about a merchant going about his business at night; it was the only time vehicles were allowed to circulate through the streets. Traffic was restricted during the day to avoid accidents.

"Good evening," said a soldier passing by with his troop of about ten soldiers. "Everything okay?"

Gallien forced a smile. "Yes, yes, fine. Thank you."

"Good night, then!"

"Yes, yes, good night!"

Gallien waited until the troop had turned the corner before pushing his cart back beneath the fig tree, climbing up, and grabbing the branch again. He gave a little hop to give himself momentum. Once, twice... finally, the fifth time, he managed to get an elbow over the branch. He gritted his teeth, grasped with all his might, and threw one leg over the branch.

Hanging there lopsided with his potbelly in the way, Gallien cursed himself for not watching his waistline these last few years. But with much perseverance, grumbling, and contortion, he was at last sitting astride the branch. With one leg to each side and both hands holding on before him, he slowly shimmied his way to the wall of the house. He landed heavily on the roof terrace and dropped down on all fours, craning his neck to scan his surroundings. Titus' was the third house down from this one. Almost all the rooftops adjoined one another. So Gallien thought it wouldn't be too difficult to move from one to the other.

Gallien crouched and moved clumsily across the rooftops. At the slightest sound of a voice or a footstep, he flopped down unceremoniously on his belly. As soon as it was quiet again, he hurried back to his feet. He was indeed in a hurry to steal the goblet before he changed his mind.

When he arrived at the house of Flavius Octavius, Gallien peered over the edge of the rooftop and into the atrium below. He stretched so far forward to get a good look that he almost lost his balance. He caught himself on the roof ledge, stifling a loud curse, but not before spotting the darkest corner of the atrium. He decided to head there.

He shifted one leg over the ledge, then the other, and tried to slip down to the ground gently. But Gallien dropped down like a sack of potatoes.

He remained crouched down for a moment, rubbing his ankle and looking around him. But how stupid—he couldn't remember where Titus' bedroom was. He should have paid more attention when he had visited him that morning.

Gallien stood up and limped toward the first room. The door was slightly ajar. Everything was quiet within—not the slightest snore. Gallien stuck his head around the door, then withdrew. That wasn't the room. He felt his way forward in the dark. Suddenly, he stubbed his toe against a chest in the hallway.

"Owww!!" he moaned.

His voice echoed loudly in the silence of the atrium.

The sound of rustling clothing came from the next room. Gallien froze. Suddenly, he rushed forward and tried to open one door, then the next.

"Hey!" a voice suddenly shouted from the back of the atrium.

At last, the third door opened, and Gallien hurriedly slipped inside.

XLIII

EMPTY!

Septimus was ripping the covers off the bed when a noise from the other side of the door made him jump. He listened, then looked quickly around for some way out of the room without being caught. He looked to the window facing the street, but it was blocked by shutters.

"Owww!" he heard someone moan.

He tried to open the shutters, but they did not unlatch easily.

"What terrible luck to get caught!" he thought in a rage. "And for nothing!"

It would be for nothing because Titus' bedroom was empty. The boy wasn't at home.

Just as the shutters finally opened, a short, round shadow slipped into the room. Septimus didn't wait to see it was Gallien; in a flash he jumped through the window and landed safely outside. Not knowing who the man was or why he was fleeing, Gallien too made a run for it. He heaved himself through the window, and plopped onto the street.

"Owww!!" he again moaned.

Gallien ran as fast as his legs would carry him. When he at last got back to his cart, his heart was beating so fast he thought it might explode. He sat down on the cart, which creaked under his weight, to catch his breath.

"I'm not young enough for this anymore," he thought, wiping the sweat from his brow with his sleeve. "I'll pay whatever Titus asks. It's less risky."

XLIV

ALERT!

Faustus rushed into Titus' bedroom. A slave had alerted him of a break-in. He had been sound asleep and hadn't heard a thing.

Everything was in place in Titus' room. Nothing had been stolen. On the other hand, the boy's bedding had been pulled apart. The pillows and blankets were strewn on the floor, as though someone had hastily gotten out of bed, or as though someone had been checking if anyone were asleep under the covers.

Faustus looked at the window. One of the shutters was open. That must be where the intruder escaped, he thought. He had been spotted in the atrium, where he had made some noise, and then he was seen entering Titus' room. Was he a thief? A murderer? The mere thought of an intruder made Faustus shiver. There had been far too many upsetting events recently for his taste. Whatever would happen next?

The old man inspected the room again in the hope of finding a clue. He put the covers and the pillows back on the bed. He patted the cushions and smoothed the sheets. That calmed him down.

Tomorrow, he would contact the *urbaniciani*. He didn't know where they were in their inquiries, but it was high time they redoubled their efforts to ensure the safety of Titus and all the members of the household. Fortunately, the boy had gone to stay at the house of Maximus. At least there he would be safe.

Faustus went to the window, and, as he leaned out to close the shutter, he heard a familiar noise. It was the clicking of swords and bucklers. He smiled. That was a lucky coincidence! A small troop of well-armed soldiers was advancing down the street. Faustus called to them from the window. "Thank goodness you're here!"

Centurion Sertor turned around with annoyance. He had more important things to worry about that night. But when he recognized the house of Flavius Octavius and his old steward, his scowl softened to a respectful smile.

"Thank goodness you're here," Faustus repeated. "We've just had an intruder in the house. He got into the room of my master's son and escaped through the window. I don't know how he got in. From the roof, I suppose."

Centurion Sertor ground his teeth. Not that same accursed case again!

"Did they do much damage?" he asked.

Faustus shook his head. "At first glance, nothing has been stolen and no one has been hurt. Thank goodness, Titus is staying at the house of his friend Maximus. But I'm extremely worried."

The centurion relaxed.

"If there's been no serious harm done," he said. "We'll come see you tomorrow. We're on another case tonight."

That made Faustus' blood boil.

"On another case?!" he growled. "That's twice now you've been busy 'on another case' when we needed you. This will be the second time you arrived too late, when all the proof was gone. Either you come in here immediately and search for clues, or you'll never have another case again! My master, Flavius

Octavius, will see to it with the emperor that you never forget this night."

The centurion gulped. These didn't sound like empty threats. But whether they were or not, Sertor couldn't afford to call his bluff. He signaled to his men.

"All right, on the double, let's go inspect this house," he shouted. "If we're quick, we can still be on time for our other mission."

Faustus smiled with satisfaction as he watched the small troop enter the house. Now that they were finally there, he would make sure they combed the whole house and detected every clue.

XLV

A VERY BUSY NIGHT

In the room he was sharing with Maximus, Titus was sound asleep, blissfully unaware that he had just escaped the clutches of Septimus. His head lay on the pillow, a smile on his sleeping face. He was dreaming about what he would buy with the money from Gallien. Maybe he would share a little with Maximus, but he hadn't decided yet. After all, it had been Maximus' fault that they had gotten into such a risky situation in the first place, and Titus still held it against him.

But before he could do anything with his money, he first had to hand the goblet over to Gallien. Then, when this whole episode was a distant memory, maybe he would come clean to his friend about the deal he had struck with the merchant.

Next to Titus, Dux too was sleeping, rolled up in a ball on the bedspread. His monkey face twitched with funny little grimaces. Was he dreaming too? Suddenly, his features froze. The animal opened one eye and sat up. There was a shadowy form in the bedroom, silently moving near Maximus' bed. Dux gave a little squeal, shook his head, rolled back into a ball, and put his little hands over his ears.

The shadow now sidled along the wall in the pale moonlight, feeling his way in the darkness. Something fell. The shadow froze.

Titus gave a grunt in his bed. He rolled over, dragging his blanket over Dux's head. Little by little, his breathing became even again.

The shadow again moved. He hit his foot against a chest by the wall. The shadow leaned over it and, with great care, eased it open. He was in luck: the hinges didn't squeak. The intruder plunged his hands into the chest and quickly found what he was looking for. A rounded object, not very big. He took the goblet out, put everything back in place, and closed the chest. The longer it took anyone to notice the goblet was missing, the better.

XLVI

A FRIENDLY WARNING

"Maximus! Titus!" shouted Aghiles.

The two boys woke with a start. It was barely daylight outside.

"What's going on?" Maximus asked, still half asleep. "Do you know what time it is?!"

"Faustus is asking to see you."

"Faustus?" asked Titus, struggling to open his eyes. "What's he doing here?"

Aghiles shrugged his shoulders. "I don't know, but he looks worried to me. Like he hasn't slept all night."

Maximus sat straight up in bed. Titus did the same, pulling the blanket off Dux.

"Tell him to come in," Maximus said to Aghiles.

Hardly a minute later, Faustus entered the room. Aghiles was right: the old man looked extremely concerned. He rushed to Titus and hugged him a little too tightly to his chest.

"Oh, my boy! You're all right. What a relief!"

"Come, come, Faustus..."

Titus freed himself from his embrace, embarrassed by such a display of emotion. At fourteen, he was almost a grown man and didn't easily let anyone hug him like that—except his mother sometimes.

"I haven't slept a wink all night," the old man said with a sigh. "I was afraid something might have happened to you."

Titus went pale.

"Why? What's happened?" Maximus asked.

"Someone broke into Flavius Octavius' house last night."

"A thief?"

"I thought so. Or, at least, I hoped so."

"That's crazy. What do you mean?"

"He didn't take anything, didn't touch anything, nothing at all."

"Then why all the worry?" Titus asked, regaining his color.

"He got into your bedroom and undid your bed," Faustus explained. "I think he must have been after you."

The blood once again drained from Titus' face. "After me?!" he stammered.

"So you see, I'm not at all reassured," Faustus exclaimed. "There have been too many strange goings-on these last couple of days. Last night, I finally managed to have a troop of the *urbaniciani* search the house. But they're totally useless. They didn't find anything, not one clue. But, I mean, you don't just force your way into someone's house without leaving a trace!"

"Well, maybe..."

"They're still searching. And believe me, I'm not letting them leave until they have a lead. In the meantime, Maximus!"

"Yes, Faustus?"

"Would you ask your parents if Titus can stay a few days with you until we get all this cleared up? I'd feel happier knowing he was safe here with you."

"Of course, Faustus. You know my parents. That won't be any problem."

"Thank you, thank you, my boy." He shook Maximus' hand with gratitude.

Then he turned to Titus. "I can't wait until your father gets back," he said. "If I were a young man, I'd sort all this out myself. But I'm just too old."

Titus shot his friends a long, meaningful glance. Maximus and Aghiles immediately understood: it was time this whole affair came to an end. They would give the goblet to Gallien and say no more about it. For the moment, Titus didn't care if the merchant paid him or not. He could have the goblet free and clear, for all he cared. All he wanted was to get rid of the thing and be done with it.

XLVII

IT'S GONE!

As soon as Faustus left, Titus shouted, "Let's hurry up and give the goblet to Gallien. Then this will all be over."

"When is he coming?" asked Maximus.

"He already came yesterday. Talk about coincidence. But he may visit again this morning."

"At your house?"

"I'm not sure..."

There was a knock on the door.

"Yes?" said Maximus.

A slave entered. "There's a gentleman at the door asking to see you."

Maximus smiled. "What does he look like?"

The slave hesitated. How could he put it diplomatically? "Not very tall," he ventured. "And... um... a bit plump."

"Our friend is an early bird," Maximus said with a grin. Then, speaking to the slave, he added, "Show him in. We were expecting him."

Hardly had Maximus spoken, when Gallien was standing before them.

"My dear friends," he gushingly greeted them.

The three boys noted with amusement the particular attention Gallien had paid to his appearance. As when he had visited Titus, he was wearing shabby clothes. Rather badly turned out, his hair tousled, Gallien made a pitiful sight. But his potbelly and fat little fingers betrayed his wealth. Another clue was that Gallien had forgotten to put on his old sandals. The ones he was wearing were fashionably new and impeccably polished— totally out of keeping with the rest of his appearance.

"This is a fine day," Gallien went on a little too eagerly, so delighted was he at the prospect of the deal he was about to conclude.

"Indeed, indeed," Titus said curtly, wanting to get to the point as soon as possible. The burden of the goblet was making him extremely nervous.

"I've brought what you asked for," he whispered to Titus with a knowing wink.

Maximus looked at Titus in bewilderment. Titus gave an embarrassed little cough.

"Yes," Titus confirmed. "As we'd decided, I asked Gallien for a little reward for having found the goblet."

Maximus frowned, still trying to understand. Aghiles took a step closer, curious to hear what Titus had to say for himself.

"You know... when we went to get it back from Septimus." Titus rolled his eyes at his friends.

"From Septimus?" Maximus asked with surprise.

"Yes. And from his men..."

Gallien observed the boys with suspicion. "You... You haven't...," he worriedly asked.

Titus elbowed Maximus in the ribs.

"Oh, no," Maximus said as he jumped and affected a broad smile. "It's just that we'd agreed not to speak to anyone about it."

"We didn't want to draw attention to ourselves," Titus added with relief.

"And...?" Gallien encouraged him.

"Ah yes," Titus sighed. "I just couldn't help myself." He turned to his friend. "Forgive me, Maximus."

Reassured, Gallien took out his purse bulging with sesterces.

"Three thousand, we said. That's right, isn't it?" he asked with a conspiratorial smile.

Maximus' eyes almost popped out of his head. Titus hadn't been shy! And yet his friend was frowning. The amount agreed was a little more than that, but Titus decided not to say anything. He knew his friends would give him a lecture, and he didn't want to make things worse.

"Perfect, perfect," he said. "And now, the goblet."

Titus took on a solemn look and went slowly to the chest placed against the wall.

"We hid it here until we saw you again," he explained. "It seemed safer to keep it here in Maximus' house, since Septimus had already paid a visit to my house."

As he spoke, Titus opened the chest and plunged his hand inside. He felt back and forth through the linens and then turned to look at his friends with a worried look on his face. Maximus stepped up to him. Gallien was craning his neck trying to get a look.

Titus went on searching more and more frantically. Maximus knelt down next to Titus and stuck his hands into the chest. He then feverishly started pulling out all the clothing and linens one by one. Soon the entire contents of the chest were on the floor. They had to face facts: the goblet was gone.

"B-b-but how...?" Titus stuttered.

"It was here yesterday evening," Maximus mumbled.

Gallien went pale, then screwing up his lips in a nasty sneer, he pulled his purse back.

"You thought you could pull one over on me," he snarled. His friendly, round face had suddenly darkened.

"No, no, not at all. I swear," Titus blurted out in confusion. "We both slept in this room, Maximus and I. Someone must have gotten in..."

"I didn't hear anything," said Maximus.

"Neither did I."

Gallien looked from one to the other with a suspicious eye. "You already took advantage of me once before," he said, his voice quivering with anger.

"It's not what you think," Titus said apologetically.

"I only think what my eyes tell me!"

"Me too," Aghiles suddenly intervened.

The other three turned to him, surprised to hear his voice.

"Yesterday, I saw a man in front of the house. He looked familiar."

"Septimus?" Titus asked with worry.

"No. The first time I saw him was the day that man who was murdered asked us for directions."

"Delitilis?" Maximus interrupted him.

Aghiles raised an eyebrow in confusion. "Delitilis?" he asked. "Who are you talking about?"

Maximus bit his lip. Ouch—he had already said too much. He feigned innocence. "I found out that the murdered man was called Delitilis."

"That's right," Gallien confirmed. "It was he who brought that goblet here to Rome."

"And what does this Delitilis have to do with what went on during the night?" Titus grumbled. "He's been dead for two days already!"

"Yesterday," Aghiles continued, "in front of the house, I spotted the man who was following Delitilis the first time we saw him. Probably the same man who killed him later..."

"You're saying he was here in front of the house?" Maximus asked.

Aghiles nodded.

"And can you tell us what he looked like?"

"I saw him better this time. He was tall. Broad-shouldered. Square-jawed. And it looked like he had one weird eye, slightly droopier than the other, I'd say."

Maximus went pale. Aghiles' description corresponded in every particular to Tiburtius, the man he had seen at Antimus' house, standing guard over him.

XLVIII

AN AMBUSH

Aghiles was about to leave when Titus caught up with him in the *vestibulum*.

"Aghiles!" he called out.

The tall Numidian turned around.

"Could you do me a favor while you're at my house?" Titus asked.

Aghiles nodded.

"Ask in the kitchen for some dates," Titus continued, looking over his shoulder to make sure Maximus couldn't overhear. "And offer them before our household gods."

Aghiles smiled. "But I don't belong to your household."

"I know, I know. But you're religious, aren't you? You believe in the spirits, the gods! People in your country are religious, aren't they?"

Aghiles didn't reply, but his eyes shone with nostalgia for his homeland.

"My household gods will listen to you. Even if they're not the same as your gods. You know I can't ask Maximus."

"Okay, I'll do it."

Titus gave a sigh of relief. "Thank you, my friend. That will make me feel much better."

With that, Aghiles left for the house of Flavius Octavius to collect Titus' things. Titus would be staying several days with

Maximus. He would need a change of clothes. To avoid Titus making the trip himself, and to reassure Faustus, Aghiles had offered to do this errand.

The walk to Flavius Octavius' house wasn't very long and was pretty direct. But at this hour of day, the streets were already crowded. So Aghiles decided to take a slight detour by way of the quieter streets. He didn't like crowds. When he would go to the Forum with his friends, he always felt as though he were suffocating. For someone from a land of wide, open spaces, many people jostling each other in a narrow street was very unpleasant.

Aghiles walked at a quick pace. He had just turned down a little side street when someone grabbed him from behind.

"Don't turn around," said a familiar voice.

Aghiles could feel the point of a knife in his back, between his ribs. "What do you want?" he asked in a husky voice.

"What do you think?"

Aghiles gulped. "We don't have it anymore."

The knife stuck in a little deeper. Aghiles didn't dare move.

"You're lying!" said the man.

"No, it's the truth."

"You stole it from me!" shouted Septimus, enraged.

"You were in no condition to take care of it," Aghiles noted with a hint of a smile.

"What?"

Again, the knife dug in a little deeper. Aghiles grimaced. The point must have pierced his skin. He could feel something warm trickling down his back.

"Someone stole it from us," Aghiles said. "Last night."

"Argh! You're lying!"

"We thought the thief must be you."

The pressure of the knife eased a little. Aghiles rapidly considered his options. If he turned around and tried to punch Septimus in the face, he had practically no chance. He was no match for Septimus, and he wouldn't get lucky twice, as he did the last time. He must break free and run for it,

"Where was it when it was stolen?" Septimus continued, again pushing in the blade.

"Maximus hid it in a chest in his room. This morning we were supposed to sell it to a dealer."

"A dealer?"

Aghiles nodded.

"What's his name?"

"Gallien."

"And you say the goblet wasn't where Maximus hid it?"

Aghiles sensed that this development had confused Septimus. He was thinking. As he did so, Aghiles took a deep breath, twisted free of the man's grip, and ran away as fast as he could.

Septimus had been caught off guard, but it only took a split second before he was in pursuit of the slave. He had an advantage over Aghiles: his training. As a former athlete, he had stayed in shape. When he wasn't caught up in business like this, he spent much of his time at the gymnasium.

But the friend of Titus and Maximus had a few things in his favor too. To start with, he knew this neighborhood like the back of his hand. Having walked up and down these streets many times, he knew every alleyway and passage. And he had stamina too, a lot of stamina. In his country, all the men and children ran long distances. If he could maintain his lead on Septimus, he would wear him out in the end.

But then, how long would it be before the ex-gladiator counterattacked?

XLIX

IN HOT PURSUIT

Septimus was fuming. He had been hoodwinked, and by a slave, a kid even! The ex-gladiator ran fast, very fast indeed. But as soon as he had made up some ground between them, Aghiles would make a sudden turn and switch direction. Having found his pace, with each turn Aghiles gained a few milliseconds, increasing his lead on Septimus.

Aghiles knew exactly where he was going. To the right, then right again, and then left. He veered in and out of a porch at top speed, moving with remarkable ease through the columns.

Septimus began to wonder if he would ever catch up with him. This rascal, he thought, was not only agile, he had unusual endurance. He wasn't showing the slightest sign of fatigue.

And yet, turning again down an alleyway, Aghiles suddenly came to a halt. A cart loaded with amphoras full of wine was blocking the narrow road. Aghiles could go neither forward nor backward. Behind him, Septimus was quickly approaching. The slave didn't have time to think. He jumped onto the cart.

Septimus surged forward, grabbed Aghiles by the leg, and pulled him with all his might. Aghiles tried kicking him with his other leg, but Septimus grabbed that one too and began pulling even harder. Aghiles held on to the cart, but he felt as though he were being ripped in two.

For Septimus, it was no longer a question of making Aghiles talk; all he wanted was revenge—to pulverize the boy and make him pay for the last few days.

Aghiles gritted his teeth. He let go of the cart with one hand and used it to shove one of the amphoras toward Septimus. It was his only chance.

The amphora rolled off the cart and smashed to pieces at Septimus' feet. The gladiator was splashed with wine. Before he had time to realize what was happening, the whole pyramid of amphoras came loose. The clay vessels rolled one after the other onto Septimus.

"Aaagh!" he cried as he fell over, letting go of Aghiles. An amphora hit him on the back of the neck at the top of his spine.

Aghiles crawled over the top of the cart. He jumped down on the other side and disappeared around the street corner.

Aghiles kept on running as Septimus lay collapsed at the foot of the cart. His neck broken, the ex-gladiator would never get up again.

Aghiles put as much distance as possible between himself and his attacker. When he at last felt safe, Aghiles stopped under a porch. Bent double with his hands on his knees and his head down, he struggled to catch his breath. His heartbeat slowly calmed down, and the blood stopped throbbing in his temples.

At last, he straightened up. That's when he saw him.

L

A PANG OF CONSCIENCE

Maximus had made up his mind, and there was no turning back. To give up now would be like admitting he had been wrong from the start. He raised his fist and knocked at the door. There was no answer. He knocked again a little harder and listened closely. He thought he could hear someone moving inside.

He leaned forward and, pressing his lips right up to the door, whispered, "It's Maximus. Let me in. I'm here to see Antimus."

No reply.

He took a step back and observed the housefront. There was no other way in. He had to see Antimus at all costs—and immediately.

He knocked again. He gave his name. Still nothing.

He wrung his hands, walked a few steps back and forth in front of the door, stopped, and then left. He was torn about what to do.

Suddenly, at the street corner, a man ran forward. When he spotted Maximus, he slowed his pace, and then he thought better of it. This was no time to get lost in second-guessing. If Antimus trusted this boy, he would trust him too. The quicker he finished with him, the quicker he could speak to Antimus.

"Maximus?" he asked from behind him.

Maximus jumped. He turned to see the face of Tiburtius looking down at him. He smiled with relief.

"I've come to see Antimus," he said. "It's very important."

Tiburtius stared at the boy a moment. His face looked different, as though he were going through some inner turmoil.

"Really," Maximus insisted, "very important."

Tiburtius cast a glance around them. This morning, he found the atmosphere of the city even less hospitable than ever.

"We don't have much time," he said at last, opening the door. "Come in."

Maximus hesitated a moment before following him inside.

Just a few yards away in the street, Aghiles stood watching in stupefaction. Maximus? Here? With that man? He shook his head. It wasn't possible; he must be dreaming, unless Maximus were there by force. But Aghiles had seen it with his own eyes: Maximus arriving, knocking at the door, calling. He had even seen him smiling at that murderer. A shiver ran down his spine and froze his blood. He couldn't understand what was happening or what he should do. At the same time, he was filled with a terrible feeling of betrayal. His friend—his best friend—had clearly been playing a double game.

LI

TAKING STOCK

Tiburtius eased the door open before shutting it quickly behind them.

"He isn't here?" Maximus asked with worry as he felt his determination fading.

"Yes, he is. But he can't receive you at the moment."

"Why not?"

"He's praying."

"Praying!?"

Incredible! Maximus needed urgently to see Antimus, and now he must wait because the man was at prayer? That was the limit. He was deeply annoyed and ready to walk out. But Tiburtius stopped him.

"Be patient. He won't be long."

Maximus scowled.

Tiburtius was trying to stall him. And at the same time, he wanted to learn more about this boy. "So, you met Antimus on a boat, did you?" he asked.

"Yes, we sailed together from Leptis Magna," Maximus grumbled.

"Do you know why he was traveling to Rome?"

Maximus relaxed. "No," he admitted. "He called himself Justinian then and said he was going to visit his family."

"And you knew he was..." Tiburtius hesitated.

"A Christian? No. At least, not at first. At first, we took him for a thief."

"A thief!?"

"But then, I began to have my doubts."

"How do you mean?"

"It was his attitude... the way he behaved. He was calm, composed. He never asked for anything and was always helpful. I've rarely seen anyone so attentive to others."

"That's true." Tiburtius sighed, lost in thought. Then he raised his head, looked Maximus straight in the eyes, and asked, "Are you a Christian too?"

Maximus laughed. "Me? A Christian? Most certainly not!"

"But then, why didn't you denounce Antimus as soon as you got off the boat, if you knew he was a Christian?"

"Why should I have?" Maximus asked. "After all, he hadn't done me any wrong."

"Fair enough. But not everyone would have reacted the same way."

"Antimus won my respect. I admired the way he dealt with things, even if I didn't agree with his beliefs. I don't care a fig about all these religious matters. I consider all that...," Maximus searched for the right word, "a waste of time."

Tiburtius gave a knowing smile. "I used to feel the same as you," he said. "I was even very anti-religious."

"And now...?"

"And now, I'm a Christian too. Funny, isn't it?"

"But then, how...?" Maximus couldn't refrain from asking out of curiosity.

"I used to be a gladiator," Tiburtius began. "And a good glad-iator at that. Then I came across a little group of Christians about to be sent to their death in the arena. Among them, there was an incredibly beautiful young woman." Tiburtius' eyes dimmed in reverie. "I immediately fell in love with her. I took her aside for a moment and offered to save her. That would have been easy for me. I knew every nook and cranny of the Colosseum. No one would even have noticed her absence."

Tiburtius broke off. Lost in his memories, he didn't even realize he had stopped speaking.

"And then?" Maximus encouraged him.

"She refused," Tiburtius recalled. "'I'm not afraid of dying,' she told me. 'Happiness awaits me. I'm ready. Save instead those who are not.' I didn't understand what she meant, and I was outraged. But the next day, at the end of a combat I was winning, when I was at the point of finishing off my opponent lying on the ground before me, I recalled her words. I looked at the man I was about to kill. He was terrified, with nothing like the serenity of that young woman. He wasn't ready to die. So I spared him."

Tiburtius fell silent for a few seconds before continuing. "The spectators booed at me and threw stones. One of them even almost put my eye out."

He smiled.

"But I've never regretted it. That very day, I looked for a way to quit as a gladiator and find out about that young woman's religion. A Christian with some money paid to free me from my contract. I've never touched a weapon since that day."

Maximus looked at him for a long moment, then took a deep breath before asking him: "But wasn't it you who murdered Delitilis? My slave saw you in front of Titus' house when Delitilis stopped to ask us for directions."

Tiburtius quaked. "Delitilis?" he asked.

"Or don't you consider a little cord around the neck to be a weapon?" Maximus continued, spurred on by the man's discomfort.

Tiburtius pulled himself up to his full height. He towered over Maximus, who was suddenly regretting having brought up the subject.

"I did not kill Delitilis!" the ex-gladiator thundered. "I give you my solemn word. I'd give up my own life to get back the Holy Chalice, but I would not kill for it. I'd die for it, but not kill!"

The force of conviction in Tiburtius' tone of voice was convincing. Maximus at once felt terrible for having made such an accusation.

"I'm so sorry," he murmured. "I thought..."

"If you're looking for the killer, look instead to Septimus. It was certainly no coincidence that the very day after the murder he passed himself off as one of the *urbaniciani*. And, in fact, he got what he wanted. It's he who got the Holy Chalice," he went on, "while I would have given my life to return it to Antimus."

Maximus remained silent. Then, he suddenly rose to his feet. "I must go," he said. "Can you give something to Antimus for me?"

"But he won't be much longer. His prayers—"

"No, I can't wait any longer. I know you'll be careful to make sure he gets it."

Tiburtius nodded. "If you wish."

At that moment, they were interrupted by a knock at the door.

"They're coming, they're coming!" someone shouted from outside.

LII

AN INDISCRETION

A disturbance suddenly roused the man from his dreams. He looked up and saw a slim, very blond boy jumping onto his roof terrace. He had come from the house next door, where there were endless comings and goings every day. Even in the night, he could hear people going in and out of that house.

He had come across the owner several times. He was a very amiable, dark-complexioned man who had only recently arrived in Rome. The neighbor wondered how such a newcomer in town could already have so many acquaintances.

From the atrium where he had been snoozing, he watched the boy who couldn't see him. The boy hesitated, looked down at the street, and then suddenly made up his mind. He gathered his strength and jumped.

Within a second, the boy had disappeared. It all happened so fast, the man wondered if he had dreamt it. But no, he was sure he had seen the boy. And he was just as sure that he recognized him. His build, the color of his hair—that could only have been the son of Julius Claudius. The man gave a nasty little laugh. What was the son of his fiercest competitor doing on the roof of his house?

LIII

SOLDIERS!

"Quick! We must leave!" said Tiburtius as he burst into the room where Antimus was still deep in prayer.

Tiburtius didn't give him time to think about it. He seized him by the collar, stood him up, and pushed him out of the room.

"They're coming!" was his only explanation. "You'll have to get out over the rooftop."

"And you?"

"I'm staying."

"Come with me. There's still time."

"No. If they find no one here, they'll search the whole house. They'll soon realize we've escaped by the roof. They'll find us. Hurry up!"

They could hear the soldiers' footsteps approaching down the street. It was hard to say how many there were.

Antimus resisted. "Don't be silly. I'm staying with you."

"But we need you!"

"There will be other priests after me."

But Tiburtius refused to listen. As Antimus argued, he clapped an object to his chest.

"Here, take that and go!"

"But what is this...?"

"Don't ask questions," Tiburtius gravely replied. "Just take it and get out of here!"

Then, with almost superhuman strength, he grabbed Antimus by the scruff of the neck and heaved him up toward the roof. "Save yourself!" he cried in a broken voice.

Antimus looked him intently in the eyes and nodded. He stretched his hands toward Tiburtius in blessing, and then he fled.

The moment he jumped onto the neighboring roof, he could hear the shout echoing in the street. "By order of the emperor, open up!"

Antimus shivered but tried not to think of his friend. Tiburtius wouldn't forgive him if he let himself be taken. He leaned down to look over the street opposite where the troop had just arrived. Fortunately, it was now deserted. He gathered up his strength and jumped.

He could hear his ankle crack as he landed. An excruciating pain shot through his leg, but Antimus immediately got up. When he tried to put weight on his foot, his leg buckled. But he gritted his teeth, whispered a prayer for courage, and limped away. He had to be as quick as possible, to put as much distance between himself and the house as he could. Above all, he mustn't think about Tiburtius. He needed to concentrate on what he had to do. On that and nothing else.

LIV

THE RAID

When the door finally gave way, Sertor expected to find the house deserted. If he hadn't spent too much of the previous evening at the house of Flavius Octavius, and hadn't been called to another crime scene, where several slaves had risen up against their master and barricaded themselves inside his house, he could have arrived here in the dead of night with an element of surprise. He could have arrested all of them.

But arriving in broad daylight like this, with plenty of eyes watching them on their way and plenty of warning tongues sounding the alarm, everyone would certainly have fled. Yet his superior officer told him not to delay the raid any longer. The rumors were already circulating that it had been planned.

The centurion was wrong about no one being in the house. There, in the middle of the atrium, stood a man. He was very tall, built like an athlete, square-jawed, dark-haired, with one droopy eye. His feet were firmly planted, and his look was determined. He had been waiting for them, ready to fight, yet he was unarmed.

Once over his astonishment, the centurion raised his arm to his men who were only waiting for his signal.

"Arrest him!" he roared. "And search the house! I want these Christians caught!"

The small troop of men split in two. One group scattered around the atrium to inspect each room. The others, with Sertor in the lead, rushed at this giant confronting them.

Tiburtius charged at the first soldier and effortlessly stopped him. With one punch to the solar plexus, he sent him flying. The second soldier fared no better. As he lunged forward with his sword, Tiburtius grabbed his arm and snapped it with a kick of the knee. The soldier's weapon went clanging at Tiburtius' feet. But Tiburtius didn't pick it up; he had sworn never to touch a weapon again. Sertor ordered a third soldier to storm this colossus of a man. While this was going on, the soldiers searching the house found nothing.

Tiburtius dodged another sword stroke and lunged at his attacker. At the same time, another soldier attacked him from behind. But with a kidney blow, he managed to avoid the swipe of a blade that just brushed his thigh. Suddenly, the battle became more heated. The first soldiers were back on their feet and had returned to the charge.

Sertor shouted furious orders. To the right and the left, Tiburtius landed kicks and punches, avoiding the sword strokes whirling round his head. He grabbed one man by the collar and slammed him against the wall; he dodged a right hook and ducked just in time to avoid a fist crashing into his face. He took some blows but gave more than he got. One soldier managed to pierce his thigh with a lance, but Tiburtius felt nothing. He was like a man of steel, ignoring the pain.

He grabbed a flowerpot and threw it in the face of another attacker, who stopped dead in his tracks. But now, those who had been searching the house joined the battle. Attacked on all sides, Tiburtius still stood his ground. In his mind, he imagined Antimus rushing through the streets of Rome. He had a pretty good inkling of where he would go to hide. It wouldn't be much longer before he got there. That one thought was enough to redouble Tiburtius' strength. With a blow of the elbow, he dislocated the jaw of a guard trying to attack him from behind.

But Tiburtius was outnumbered. Despite his strength and determination, he couldn't hold them off much longer. Suddenly, he was staggered by a blow to the forehead. He gathered his wits and landed a punch on a soldier to his right. Blood was flowing from Tiburtius' scalp. He must have taken another blow to the head without realizing it. His vision started to blur. He thought of Antimus. Yes, he must have gotten there by now. Tiburtius stepped toward a soldier advancing on him with his sword. He lifted him up in one hand and smashed him against one of the atrium's pillars.

Sertor moved in from behind. He readied his sword and thrust it deep into Tiburtius' side. The colossus collapsed to his knees. Sertor stabbed him again. Tiburtius fell heavily on one side. He was done for, he knew it.

Everything was going dark around him. And yet, he smiled. He was thinking of that pretty Christian girl he had met in the Colosseum. He wasn't afraid anymore either. He now understood what she had meant. Antimus was safe, he was sure of it. Tiburtius had succeeded. And now he was ready.

LV

MAXIMUS!

Aghiles wandered through the ransacked house.

The soldiers had left empty-handed. They had taken no prisoners. But the house had been laid waste.

In the atrium lay the body of a dead man, collapsed at the base of the little fountain that went on gaily trickling. Aghiles recognized him straight away. It was the man he had seen with Maximus just a little while earlier. A shiver ran down his spine.

He was terrified by what he might discover in the other rooms. But there was nothing else in the house, no clue as to the fate of his young master. The rooms had all been turned topsy-turvy, the chests and drawers rifled through. He found blood in several places in the atrium, a sword, and a helmet left behind by one of the soldiers. But there was no other body.

"Maximus!" shouted Aghiles in a choked voice.

He had no idea where Maximus might have hidden or how he could have escaped without being seen, but he must do his level best to find out. This raid had surprised and terrified him. Like all the inhabitants of Rome, Aghiles knew only too well what this meant. Most of the time, it was a round-up of Christians who had been denounced.

"Maximus!" he now screamed.

No answer, nothing but silence in the house except for the babbling fountain.

Fraught with anxiety, Aghiles quickly forgot his earlier feelings of betrayal. Now that he feared Maximus lost, he suddenly realized he didn't know his friend as well as he had thought. As much as Maximus liked endlessly to make fun of Titus and his superstitions, perhaps he had been touched by this new religion.

The more Aghiles thought about it, the less improbable it seemed. As Aghiles understood it, the Christian religion was the complete opposite of Roman worship: one sole God, no good-luck charms or oracles, no offerings of dates to household divinities. It rejected all that Maximus hated most.

"Maximus!" he called out as he searched every nook and cranny. He searched for any other exit, a door or a window, where his friend might have escaped. But there was nothing. That left only the roof. Aghiles raised his eyes; that was the only other way his friend could have gotten out. At least, he hoped so.

"Maximus!!" he screamed.

In the house next door, the neighbor smugly smiled.

"Hmm, Maximus...," he repeated to himself. "Just as I thought..."

He had been following events from the start. First, the escape of Maximus through the roof, followed by that of the owner of the house. He had suspected he might be a Christian, with all the coming and going and tiptoeing about.

He was sure of that now, thanks to the raid.

LVI

FURY

Maximus arrived back home, out of breath but unharmed. He had run all the way without stopping, without even a glance behind him. He didn't want to know what might have happened to Antimus. Yet he was strangely at peace. He had done what he had to do.

"Maximus!" said Titus. "I was beginning to get worried."

"Sorry, it took longer than I thought."

"But you didn't find anything?" said Titus with surprise, seeing his friend return empty-handed.

"No, I didn't like anything. I still can't decide what to give her. In the end, I'm not sure she'd like a *fibula*.[1]"

"Your mother already has so many..."

Maximus nodded in agreement.

"Aghiles still isn't back yet?" Maximus asked nonchalantly to change the subject.

"Not yet. I hope nothing's happened to him. He's been such a long time."

"Stop being such a worrywart. What could have happened to him?"

"I don't know. It's just, you know, these last few days..."

---

1. A sort of broach to hold a garment in place.

Maximus made no reply. He too was worried. He didn't dare think what might have happened if he had still been in Antimus' house when the soldiers arrived.

Suddenly, there was a disturbance in the *vestibulum*.

"Maximus?" thundered a voice they barely recognized. "Is Maximus in there?"

Maximus could hear someone answer. He left the room and, in disbelief, saw Aghiles standing in the hallway looking haggard.

"Aghiles?!"

The young man raised his eyes and looked upon Maximus with relief. He had been so frightened for his friend. But then, in the blink of an eye, his expression hardened. He was angry with Maximus for giving him such a scare and for having hidden everything from his closest friends.

"Aghiles!" shouted Titus, rushing to him. "I thought something must have happened to you!"

Titus embraced his friend with relief.

"No, nothing's happened," replied Aghiles in a chilly tone. "Nothing special. I just took my time."

As he spoke, he glared at Maximus. Squirming uncomfortably, Maximus looked away. This was the first time Aghiles had ever been so mad at him.

"Thank you, thank you, my friend," continued Titus. "Thanks to you, I've got everything I need for the next few days."

Titus stopped. He looked at Aghiles with surprise.

"But didn't Faustus give you any of my things for me?" he asked.

The slave remained silent. He hadn't gone to Titus' house and had no wish to explain why. His eyes remained riveted on Maximus.

"Right. Fine," Titus replied in a cajoling voice. "No problem, I'll manage without them."

He looked at Maximus and then at Aghiles, and exclaimed, "You're both looking very strange. What's going on?"

Maximus shook his head. That was just it: he didn't know exactly what was going on. All he knew was that Aghiles was terribly angry with him and he didn't understand why.

"Stop looking like that!" Titus blurted out. "You look like you've just lost your best friend."

A cloud passed over Aghiles' face for a second.

"He knows," thought Maximus.

He felt a twinge of sorrow. He had hoped no one would suspect anything. But there was no point in crying over spilt milk. In any case, he would just have to deny everything.

LVII

DENOUNCED

"I'd like to speak to someone in charge, please," whispered the man who had just entered the barracks of the *urbaniciani.* "I have an important disclosure to make."

The soldier smiled. That's what they all said when they came to see them. And three-quarters of the time, their information was useless.

"I'm sorry, they're all out," he replied as politely as possible. "If you'd like to tell me what it's about, I'll pass on the message."

But the man wrinkled his nose. "I'll only speak to an officer in charge. I can wait."

The soldier sighed. Another one of those endless time-wasters. "He may be quite some time," he said. I can give him your message."

"No, thank you. I'll wait."

The man spotted a bench in a corner and sat down, his back as unbending as righteous justice. He gave a good look all around him, imagining the events that would now unfold over the next few days—or even in the next few hours. Just the thought of it made him smile. The gods were with him. He couldn't have dreamt of a better opportunity to get rid of Senator Julius Claudius.

After waiting for a long time, imperturbably seated on the bench in the barracks, the man noticed soldiers arriving.

"They're back," the man thought to himself. He smiled with satisfaction. Now he would be able to see an officer.

"We have no prisoners," said a returning soldier to his awaiting comrades. The men in the barracks stared at their feet. The centurion would be in a foul mood; this wasn't the time to get oneself noticed.

But the man waiting on the bench was unaware of what the policeman meant. All that mattered to him was to make his statement. Then he just had to trust in justice. This business was far too juicy not to create a scandal.

Centurion Sertor suddenly burst into the barracks. There was immediate silence. He looked furious, while the men behind him looked exhausted. Some of them were wounded.

The man on the bench jumped up and ran with little hurried steps to the officer in charge. "Centurion!" he called out.

Sertor gave a slight turn of the head and waved an angry arm. "I don't want to see anyone!"

"But, Centurion," the man insisted, "I have information that will be of great interest to you."

Centurion Sertor shot him a dirty look and continued on his way. "This is not the time!" he growled.

"But you must hear me out!"

Sertor turned on him violently. He grabbed the man by the collar, raised him up on tiptoe, and looked him straight in the eye. "Listen, unless you've got something of the utmost importance to report, which I doubt, I suggest you remember your place and get lost."

The man trembled from head to toe as great drops of sweat rolled down his forehead. "I... uh, it's just... I saw something," he squeaked.

Sertor growled and sent him flying against the wall.

Stunned a little, the man stood up slowly. But then he straightened his clothes and said, "Perhaps you'd be interested to know that a bit earlier a troop of soldiers raided my neighbor's house..."

A glimmer of interest flickered in Sertor's eyes.

"And where do you live?" he asked.

The man gave the address.

The centurion gave a snide little smile. "And you say you heard something?" he asked in a suddenly friendly voice.

The man was emboldened. It was now his move. "I didn't say I *heard* something. I said I *saw* something."

"Saw? Saw what?"

"A young man escaping over the roof. And then another one, a little older, no doubt from somewhere around Carthage."

"I knew there must be others!" Sertor stormed. He turned to the man, "And is that everything?"

"No," the man murmured with an oily grin, "it's just that..." He puffed himself up—this was surely his moment of glory.

"Come on, come on!" Sertor brusquely hurried him. "Get to the facts!"

The little man wanted to make him wait for it, but when Sertor suddenly approached him with a furious scowl, he spilled everything he knew. "I was able to identify the young man. His slight build and very blond, almost white, hair immediately made me think of the son of Senator Julius Claudius."

Sertor's eyes widened with surprise.

"And a little later, I confirmed it. After you and your men left, someone went into the house. He was looking for something, or rather *someone*. He kept calling out 'Maximus!'"

The man stopped to prolong the suspense.

"So that confirmed what I first suspected," he continued. "The son of Julius Claudius is called Maximus."

"The son of Julius Claudius?! A Christian?!" Centurion Sertor repeated, trying to take in this news. "That's unbelievable. And you're sure about all this?"

"Perfectly sure."

"If you're mistaken, you'll take his place as fodder for the lions in the arena."

The man confidently threw back his shoulders. He had just gotten rid of his main rival. Julius Claudius would never recover from this.

LVIII

THE ACCUSED

There was a strange atmosphere in Maximus' room. Titus and Maximus were playing *latroncules*, a game of strategy. Aghiles sat silently in the background. There was nothing unusual about that: he was never very talkative. But usually he took an interest in his friends' games and liked to listen to them chatting about this and that.

Leaning over the gameboard, Titus, on the contrary, was very talkative. The disappearance of the goblet seemed to have lifted a great weight from his shoulders. Now that the thief had gotten what he wanted, Titus had nothing to worry about anymore, even if Faustus didn't seem to feel the same. But the family steward was unaware even of the existence of this goblet and the many dangers it had brought into their lives. So it was normal for him to be worried about a break-in during the night for no apparent reason.

"I suppose," Titus said, "we'll probably never know who finally got it in end. My money's on Septimus. What do you think?"

"Yes, probably Septimus," Maximus agreed. He moved a piece on the gameboard and looked at his friend Aghiles sitting across from him. "But, by the way, Titus: What was that business about money with Gallien all about?"

Titus gave a nervous little cough and lowered his eyes. "I was going to talk to you about that," he replied with embarrassment.

"Were you trying to make money behind our backs?"

"It's not how you think. But I thought it was a little too easy for Gallien to get what he wanted without having to lift a finger when we took all the risks."

"That's not what you seemed to think when you criticized me for not giving him the goblet right away."

Titus blushed. "Well, in the end I changed my mind. I'm allowed to change my mind, aren't I!?"

"I think..."

Before Maximus had time to finish his sentence, the door flew open with a bang. Julius Claudius entered the room with a centurion right behind him, smiling with satisfaction. Maximus' father looked white.

"Maximus," he shouted in a strained voice. "Will you please come with me? Right now!"

In his corner, Aghiles sat bolt upright, on the alert.

Julius Claudius stretched out his hand toward him.

"No need for you to come with us, Aghiles. I need to speak to Maximus alone."

Maximus stood up, as white as a sheet. His father wasn't in the habit of summoning him like this. And never had his father been accompanied by a soldier.

He followed his father into his office. Julius Claudius took a seat, or rather flopped wearily down into an armchair. But he made no offer to his son to sit down.

"Maximus, Centurion Sertor has just told me something that has left me speechless."

Maximus turned to the soldier with a questioning look.

"Someone saw you today...," Julius Claudius began.

Maximus felt the blood draining from his face. He gulped hard.

"Someone saw you on the roof of a house."

There was silence.

"Saw you fleeing from a house where Centurion Sertor and his men had been ordered to arrest Christians."

"But I... I," Maximus tried to defend himself, knowing he was in big trouble. The facts were overwhelming.

Julius Claudius remained silent. What more was there to say? He looked at his son standing before him; his whole attitude was enough to tell him what the centurion had told him was true.

Catastrophe had struck his house. Of course, he would be required to resign as a senator, his reputation would be ruined, and his family destined for disgrace. But worst of all, his dear son, his only son, would be condemned and thrown to the lions like all those other Christians stirring up trouble in the country. And to think that his son had always been so uninterested in anything religious!

"But it's not true! This can't be happening!" Maximus cried in despair.

LIX

WITNESSES

Maximus' friends, Titus and Aghiles, were his last chance. They were the only ones who could prove his innocence and save him. Maximus trusted in their friendship. He had to. They were his only hope.

"Ask my friends," he whimpered. "We haven't left each other's side."

Julius Claudius gave his son a long look. A faint glimmer of hope lit his eyes. If only he could believe his son was telling the truth.

Centurion Sertor ground his teeth. For him, the case was clear. What use was there in adding more witness statements that would only confirm what he already knew?

"Centurion," Julius Octavius pleaded, "I beg you, give my son the benefit of the doubt. Ask his friends."

Sertor considered. He couldn't allow the slightest error in this case. Julius Claudius was too important a man. Sertor couldn't afford any criticism in his handling of the case.

"So be it," he grudgingly agreed. "I'll question them."

Maximus breathed a little more easily.

"But individually," the centurion added with a smirk.

Maximus closed his eyes. All he could do now was to trust that his friends would understand.

The centurion called Aghiles in first. It was a quick interrogation. Aghiles wasn't talkative, and Centurion Sertor didn't attach much credence to what he had to say. After all, he was a slave. His statements mattered little under Roman law.

When the centurion then summoned Titus, the boy was immediately nervous. He was ready to admit anything and everything right away. Yes, the goblet had been in their possession. No, they didn't have it anymore. Yes, it had been stolen. No, they never intended to keep it or even to sell it, but simply to bring it to the emperor.

But, as soon as the interrogation began, Titus realized that the soldier before him knew nothing about any goblet, not even that one existed. All he was interested in was Maximus. So Titus understood that his friend was in danger. And that one thought suddenly gave him courage, an unusual thing for someone who was normally such a scaredy-cat.

"Where was your friend Maximus today?"

Titus thought fast.

"At home," he replied trying to gain time.

He thought again about Maximus, who had gone out shopping but come back empty-handed. He suddenly found that strange.

"And he remained here the whole time?"

"Of course, we were playing *latroncules*. It's our favorite game."

"And you were playing the whole day?"

"Ah, well, you know how it is, once you start playing...," Titus answered with increasing boldness.

"And he didn't go out?"

"No."

"He was here the whole time with you?"

"Yes."

Centurion Sertor was troubled. This wasn't at all what he had been hoping to hear. The slave had told him the same thing, but he hadn't given much weight to what he said. But this time, with Titus, it was different. He was the son of Flavius Octavius, a very prominent and respected man.

He tried another approach, hoping to intimidate the boy.

"What if I told you that Maximus is a Christian?" he asked in a threatening tone.

Titus' laughter totally threw him.

"Maximus? A Christian?" Titus guffawed. "You must be joking!"

After the tension of the last few moments, Titus broke into uncontrollable giggles. He struggled to regain a straight face.

"Honestly," he continued, "it's clear you don't know Maximus."

"Meaning?"

"Meaning I don't know anyone less religious than he is."

Titus bit his lip and suddenly stopped laughing. He was afraid he had said too much.

"Excuse me, I'm sorry... That's not quite what I meant to say. He respects the emperor and the Roman gods, but he's not a great practitioner. He doesn't pray or make offerings beyond what's required of a good Roman citizen."

With that, Centurion Sertor got to his feet. He had heard enough. He dismissed Titus, who left the room.

"Well, centurion?" Julius Claudius asked him hopefully.

Sertor paused before answering. What he had to say galled him.

"For the moment, the boys' statements are consistent," Sertor said. "The three of them claim that they were together here all day. I'll have to question them again, but not right away. I need to clear up a few details first."

"And my son?"

"Your son?"

"Yes, Maximus."

"What about him? "

"Are you taking him in?" Julius Claudius worriedly asked.

"Not yet. But I'm placing him under house arrest. I'll have a soldier posted outside your door. He's forbidden to go out."

An enormous weight lifted from the shoulders of Julius Claudius. It was too good to be true.

LX

A CONFESSION

"Oh, my friends, my friends!" said Maximus as he rushed to Titus and Aghiles and hugged them. He had been right to trust in their friendship.

"But what in the world is this all about?" asked Titus, feigning indignation. "I had to tell him you didn't go out all day."

Titus gave him a half-amused, half-curious smile. He was itching to know what was going on.

Next to him, Aghiles had lost his frostiness. He too was smiling. Maximus had been within a whisker of serious trouble. And, after all, everyone is free to have his own beliefs.

"You know what's the funniest thing about this?" Titus asked.

"No."

"The centurion asked me if you were a Christian. You! A Christian! Ha!"

Maximus gave a hollow laugh. "Indeed, that's an odd question," he said. "But I owe you an explanation."

Maximus was about to begin, when Aghiles interrupted him. "Me too, Maximus, I'd like to know if you're a Christian."

Titus looked at him with amusement. But his smile disappeared as he realized Aghiles was being serious. "Aghiles, what are you trying to say?"

"I'd like to know if Maximus is a Christian or not," repeated Aghiles without taking his eyes off Maximus.

"Oh, come on, that's ridiculous," said Titus.

"No, it's very serious. I know where Maximus was today."

Now we get to it, thought Maximus.

"Well, I know too," Titus replied. "He was here! He didn't move the whole day. That's what I told the centurion."

"And I said the same thing," Aghiles said in a somber voice. "But I lied. Maximus..."

"Come on, Aghiles, stop this...," Titus urged.

"I'll tell you, Aghiles," Maximus said. "No, I am not a Christian."

"But then, what were you doing in that house?"

"What house?" Titus demanded.

"And with that man, the one with the droopy eye?"

"What man? What droopy eye?" Titus asked again, starting to become annoyed.

"That man's name is Tiburtius," Maximus calmly replied. "And he's not the murderer you think he is."

"What murderer?"

"And as for that house, it's where Antimus lives."

"Where he used to live, you mean," Aghiles grumbled. "Because I can tell you, it's empty now. I went there. I thought you'd been killed just like that man, that Tiburtius..."

"Tiburtius is dead?!" asked Maximus.

"What Tiburtius?!" yelled Titus. "By Jove! Are you going to tell me what you're talking about?!"

Maximus sat down. "Aghiles is right," he began in a quiet voice. "Today I went to the house where some Christians lived."

"You?" Titus couldn't believe his ears.

"It's not how you think. I went to see Antimus."

"That's the second time you've mentioned his name. But who is he?" Aghiles asked.

"Antimus is Justinian's real name."

"Justinian? The one from the boat?" Titus asked.

Maximus nodded.

"Antimus—or Justinian, if you prefer—is a Christian priest."

Titus' jaw dropped.

"I realized it on the boat, but I didn't say anything."

"But that doesn't explain why you went to see him," Titus correctly noted.

"I went to give him the goblet, what they call the Holy Chalice."

Maximus' words met with a long silence. It took Titus and Aghiles a moment to take in the full significance of what their friend had just told them.

"But... but... the goblet was stolen?"

Maximus nodded in agreement. "Yep."

"Do you know by whom?"

"By me."

"What...?!"

"I let you think it had gone missing. It was the only way to get it back to Antimus. You would never have agreed to it," said Maximus looking at Titus. "You above all wouldn't have wanted to."

"But... why did you want to?"

"Antimus told me what this goblet means to them, to the Christians. It was very moving; he was so full of hope. I didn't have the heart to give it to Gallien or anyone else who wouldn't respect that."

"But do you realize what you're saying?!" Titus was now on his feet, approaching his friend with renewed anger. "Do you realize you lied to us! That you put us in danger because of your whims! Do you realize that I gave false witness to cover up your insanity!" Titus was choking with rage. "You went about your little business all on your own without a thought for us, for what we might think, of the possible consequences for us? And then, you count on us to cover up for you to get you out of this mess?! What about trust? What about friendship? What about that, huh? You... you... you... Arghhh!"

Titus made a furious gesture, turned around and flung the door open. Just as he was leaving, he made an about-face and pointed a finger at Maximus. "Well, don't count on me anymore, do you hear! Don't count on me anymore!"

With that, he slammed the door behind him. Maximus closed his eyes. His friend's anger was justified. Then he looked to Aghiles, who slowly turned his back to him.

LXI

A COOLING-OFF PERIOD

Titus was like a caged lion. A funny way perhaps to describe the son of a wild animal trader, but, in fact, there was nothing funny about it. He roamed the house like a troubled spirit, turning recent events over and over in his mind.

It had been two days now since Titus and Maximus had seen each other. Two whole days! That had practically never happened before. The two of them had been friends for years, ever since Maximus' father had gone to Flavius Octavius to buy a sacred ibis as a present for his wife. That was more than ten years ago now.

Maximus' revelations were deeply hurtful to Titus, and for the first time, their friendship was sorely put to the test. Something seemed broken, which made Titus both furious and miserable at the same time. And to think that the cause of the break was a goblet that neither of them had sought or wanted.

For his part, Aghiles avoided Maximus the best he could. For a personal slave, that was tricky, but he got caught up in household chores and, at the slightest opportunity, volunteered for outside errands.

The tie that bound him and Maximus wasn't the same as the friendship between Maximus and Titus. It ran very deep but was more recent. And, most of all, it was colored by the master-slave relationship, even if Maximus always tried to make sure

Aghiles felt it as little as possible. But still, Aghiles' life hung on the whim of his young master. And today, he no longer felt he could have complete confidence in him. That was a very unpleasant feeling.

And as for Maximus, he quite simply felt lost. And he felt torn. He couldn't help thinking that returning the goblet to Antimus and his Christian brethren had been the right thing to do. Yet at the same time, he felt badly about lying to his friends, his father, and the police.

Forbidden from leaving the house, Maximus too was pacing in his room, counting the minutes that seemed to drag by. He who so loved action, to master events, could do nothing. He was helpless, dependent on the goodwill of others. His fate was in the hands of his friends, and he had no idea how they were reacting to what they saw as a real betrayal on his part.

Centurion Sertor was in no better frame of mind than the three boys. He had hoped that the statements of the son of Flavius Octavius and the slave would have contradicted each other and allowed him to charge Julius Claudius' son with treason. Instead, their accounts perfectly coincided.

The centurion found himself in a sticky situation. If he hoped to prove the guilt of Maximus, he would need to find another witness. The neighbor who had denounced Maximus wasn't enough. Especially not since Sertor found out that the man was a personal rival of Senator Julius Claudius. He could have made the whole thing up with the sole aim of destroying his competitor.

Titus had to do something. He was leaving the house with a determined step when he came face-to-face with Aghiles.

"I was just coming to see you," explained Aghiles.

"And I was coming to see you."

LXII

CONFLICTING TESTIMONY

As Centurion Sertor was leaving the barracks, he stopped in surprise. Two boys were outside and coming straight toward him. They had clearly been waiting for him.

"Centurion Sertor!" Titus called to him.

The officer squinted and carefully observed him. Yes, he recognized him. Who wouldn't recognize Titus with that monkey perched on his shoulder?

"How can I help you?"

The other boy—or rather the slave—also approached him.

"We'd like to reconsider our statements," Titus explained.

Sertor raised a curious eyebrow.

"To reconsider?"

"Exactly."

"Are you implying that you lied?"

Titus smiled with a little embarrassment. He wasn't overly confident, but knew he was in a position of strength. Sertor hadn't returned to question them, which must mean his investigation was stalled.

"Let's just say we didn't tell you everything."

"So...?" Sertor asked hopefully.

"We think it's time you knew what really happened before taking this affair to the emperor."

For over an hour, Titus talked. Aghiles was content just to nod in agreement. Titus told the centurion everything: Septimus, the murder, the goblet, their kidnapping, Gallien, Dux, Tiburtius, the Holy Chalice, Antimus... He left nothing out, not one location, not one name.

Sertor quickly saw that he wasn't making any of this up. Septimus, for example: the *urbaniciani* had found him dead three days ago, the victim of an accident. And someone had formally identified him as the man who had passed himself off as a member of the *urbaniciani* and questioned Titus and his friends the day after the murder.

As Titus spoke, things seemed to become clear in the centurion's mind. This painstaking investigation was suddenly coming to a conclusion. He had no reason to doubt what the boy told him. It all fit together. It all rang true. Except for one little detail...

"Maximus immediately suspected Tiburtius of having taken the Holy Chalice," Titus continued in a confident tone. "Since he knew where he lived, he wanted to go get it back."

"All on his own?" said Sertor with surprise. "That was dangerous, if that man was a Christian."

Titus shrugged his shoulders, "Danger has never stopped Maximus."

He shot a smile at Aghiles, who smiled back at him. Their eyes shone with the same glimmer of amusement as they thought of Maximus.

"You must have arrived just at that moment," Titus concluded. "In fright, he fled by the roof. I would have done the same in his place."

"No!" Aghiles interrupted.

"What do you mean, no?" asked Sertor.

"Titus wouldn't have done the same for the pure and simple reason that he could never put himself in the same place as Maximus."

Titus gave a wide smile and lowered his eyes.

"It's true, I would never have had his courage."

Sertor listened to the two boys politely bickering about their friend. With that, he rubbed his hands. He was now satisfied.

"Right, I think I've heard enough."

"You'll clear Maximus?" Titus asked nervously.

"I have no reason to pursue him further."

The two boys heaved a sigh of relief. How good it felt to know that their friend was out of danger and that all the lies they had been telling were behind them.

"Nevertheless...," the centurion said.

Aghiles looked up at him with worry.

"There still remains one question I'll unfortunately never be able to answer."

"One question?" Titus asked.

"Where on earth did that goblet end up?"

EPILOGUE

Two months later in Roman Hispania, in the region of Huesca

Antimus clutched the goblet to his heart one last time.

"You'll take good care of it?" he asked his friend.

The man smiled. "Don't you worry," he said. "Nothing will happen to it now."

Antimus handed him the goblet.

The man laid it carefully in a little casket and placed it in a hole dug under the floor. "They'll never imagine that the goblet returned to its original hiding place," he said. "They won't come looking for it here again. But you can never be too careful. This time, I prefer to bury it."

Slowly, the man covered the casket with earth. With each handful of soil, Antimus felt a little tug on his heartstrings.

Finally, the man signaled Antimus to help him. The two of them shifted a chest of linens and dishes over the hole. Unless someone had seen it, he would never know it was there.

Antimus rose with a smile. Tiburtius would be proud of him. The Holy Chalice was safe once again. He had carried out his mission to the end.

AUTHOR'S NOTE

In A.D. 258, Pope Sixtus II entrusted the Holy Chalice to Saint Lawrence just before his death. In order to protect it and keep it out of the hands of the Romans seeking to destroy it, Saint Lawrence sent the precious goblet to his family, in the region of Huesca. And there it remained hidden for years.

The Holy Chalice was surely not the object of quite so many intrigues as those in this novel. On the other hand, one thing is certain: in Valencia, not far from Huesca, the cathedral today houses a relic said to be the Holy Chalice. In 1982, Saint John Paul II himself venerated this relic and celebrated Mass with it.

The Holy Chalice in Valencia is a large goblet mounted on a gold base and set with precious gems. So nothing to do with the goblet in our story? Don't be so sure. Over the course of history, the Holy Chalice was transformed into a precious object. But beneath all the gilding and the jewels is the very simple goblet that many have believed Christ himself used—a goblet in brown agate with streaks of orange.

Printed in June 2022 by Rotolito, Italy
Job number MGN22025
Printed in compliance with
the Consumer Protection Safety Act, 2008